DEAR OBSESSION

Dr. Manley's wife Kate has allowed her son Johnnie to become an obsession, excluding the rest of her family. However, when the doctor takes a new partner, Dr. Paul Quest, everything changes. Johnnie becomes more independent and her husband less willing to go along with her obsession. Kate, now realising that she is in danger of losing her husband, must also accept the bitter truth: that Johnnie is capable of doing without her . . .

Please return on or before the latest date above.
You can renew online at *www.kent.gov.uk/libs*
or by telephone 08458 247 200

1 2 FEB 2020

CUSTOMER SERVICE EXCELLENCE

Libraries & Archives

00884\DTP\RN\07.07   LIB 7

I. M. FRESSON

DEAR OBSESSION

Complete and Unabridged

LINFORD
Leicester

First published in Great Britain in 1975 by
Robert Hale & Company
London

First Linford Edition
published 2008
by arrangement with
Robert Hale Limited
London

British Library CIP Data

Fresson, I. M.
　　Dear obsession.—Large print ed.—
　　Linford romance library
　　1. Mothers and sons—Fiction
　　2. Domestic fiction 3. Large type books
　　I. Title
　　823.9'14 [F]

　　ISBN 978–1–84782–485–1

Published by
F. A. Thorpe (Publishing)
Anstey, Leicestershire

Set by Words & Graphics Ltd.
Anstey, Leicestershire
Printed and bound in Great Britain by
T. J. International Ltd., Padstow, Cornwall

This book is printed on acid-free paper

1

Kate wondered as she cut the flowers just how much the coming of the new partner would affect their lives. Dell certainly needed help now that the number of patients had increased so much, the two estates which had developed with the building of the new road had brought many more people to the district and because of this, he was badly overworked.

She stood absentmindedly smelling a rose she had just cut. For herself, she hated change; hated everything which might disrupt Johnnie's life or make him unhappy. She laid the rose carefully in the basket with the others and moved on down the border. The garden was at its best in June and the flowers lovely. They were lucky to be in the backwater of this old house with the wooded garden. With the expanding town, there were few places left with such seclusion. That, at least, had been wonderful for Johnnie.

Frowning, Kate tried to remember Dr. Paul Quest from the only time they had met. Nearly as tall as Dell, much darker, though she couldn't recollect what sort of hair. She remembered a lean face with a determined chin. A voice deep and pleasant. Eyes? Blue or grey? She didn't know. He was, of course, much younger than Dell and she wondered just how her husband would like working with someone else after being on his own for so long, how the patients would react to a stranger. The practice had always been such a personal one, it wouldn't be easy to adjust.

If Dell had more leisure, what would he do with it? It surprised her that she had no idea and she realised with a sense of shock that she no longer knew what interested her husband outside his work. It was so long since she had been free to share that leisure because she couldn't leave Johnnie.

Kate sighed as she picked up the basket of flowers. Dell had never understood that; never understood anything about Johnnie's need of her, never been able to see that the least she could do was to devote the rest of her life to the boy. There had always been clashes between them because Dell resented her doing so much for him. Latterly, there had been few because he had seen that it was useless, but it was tacitly understood between them that he disapproved of her making their son so dependent on her. Kate sighed. No, he would never understand.

In the pantry, she began to arrange the flowers, something she loved doing.

'Nobody can make flowers look as lovely as you do.'

She turned sharply.

'Oh, Dell, you made me jump. I never heard you.'

'No. You were engrossed in your flowers. You haven't forgotten Paul is coming to dinner?'

'No. These roses are for the dinner table. Are you going out now? Would you like some tea before you leave?'

'If you've time, it would be nice.'

'Well, carry these through for me and I'll put the kettle on.'

In the kitchen, he stood drinking the tea she made, drinking it much too hot, much too fast. All part of his constant chase of time. He thought suddenly that perhaps now he might sometimes have a moment to drink a cup of tea without scalding himself. Even time for a little leisure. Leisure? What would he do with it? He had forgotten what it was like to have free time. If he'd ever had any hobbies, he didn't remember what they were.

'How do you think you will like working with a partner?'

He smiled as he put down his cup.

'It'll be strange at first but he's a nice chap and a good doctor, so I expect it will work out all right.' He turned at the door. 'I'll try to be back before he arrives if I can.'

4

Kate watched as he almost ran out to the hall, picking up his bag as he went. Perhaps it was because of the coming change in their lives, but she was seeing him more clearly than she had for a long time. He was just as handsome in his late forties as he had been when she had married him. Tall and well made, his figure good and he still walked with that controlled movement, which for some reason, had fascinated her when they first met.

Standing by the kitchen table finishing her own tea, Kate allowed her thoughts to travel back to the time when she and Dell had been so close that nothing else seemed to matter. If only life could have stood still at that point.

She put down the cup and the clatter against the saucer brought her abruptly back to the present. What nonsense was she thinking? Would she have been happy never to have had Lise? Or Johnnie. Would Dell? At least he was devoted to Lise and, she supposed, in his own way, to Johnnie. It was just that they thought so differently about the boy. So differently that there had ceased to be a touching point between them. Dell and she got on as well as most married couples. They didn't have rows. It was; she hesitated, not wanting to face her own thoughts.

Picking up the cup and saucer, she carried it over to the sink. Sighing, she completed the words in her mind. It was just that they were no longer vital to each other as they had been.

Kate heard Lise come through from the surgery and called that there was tea if she wanted it.

'Yes, good. I'll come.'

She came into the kitchen still wearing her white overall. Ever since she had left school, she had worked as her father's receptionist. A job which she enjoyed and which she did well.

'Can I help you with anything?'

'You might take Johnnie up some tea.'

Lise carried it carefully while her

6

mother watched her. Today, she seemed more aware of her daughter as well as her husband. She was glad that Lise had stayed after she left school but wondered that such an attractive girl didn't find both the job and the place too dull. There was Philip Cranston, of course, but Lise seemed in no hurry to come to any decision where he was concerned. Perhaps she was not in love with him after all.

Lise had inherited her mother's lovely chestnut coloured hair but otherwise, there was no resemblance to either parent. She was, Kate thought, just simply, herself, a small girl with laughing hazel eyes, a wide brow and mouth, a short nose and a chin which looked too determined for the rest of her face.

Kate smiled as she disappeared up the stairs. Lise's character matched her chin. Nothing shifted her once she had made up her mind. A blast of noise wafted down the stairs as Lise opened Johnnie's door.

He was lying on his bed, hands behind his head, listening to the pop record which beat around the room.

'What a ghastly row. Must you have it on so loud?'

He grinned up at his sister good naturedly.

'You can't get the feel of it if you don't,' he told her with mock seriousness.

'There's no tune in it, anyway.'

'Duckie, your trouble is that you're getting old. A little before your time, perhaps, but undoubtedly that must be the reason if you can't enjoy this.' Again, he smiled as he took the tea from her.

'If you can hear yourself think, don't forget that Doctor Quest is coming for dinner.'

'Oh, gosh — I had. What a bore. What time?'

'About seven, I think. I can't shout above this row any more — I'm off.'

'You know you like it really,' he said slyly as she quickly closed the door.

An hour later, Kate at her dressing-table, carefully applying make-up, reflected as she did so, that it was a long time since she had used any. Why was she bothering now? She supposed, to make a good impression on the new partner. Looking at her reflection, she had to admit that the make-up was a great improvement. She wondered vaguely why she didn't normally bother. Too tired and too little time. Who was there to appreciate what she looked like, anyway?

Dell opened the bedroom door, crossing the room to stand behind her.

'You look pretty good tonight. Do you want this thing done up?'

He zipped the back of her dress neatly and she smiled at him in the mirror. So he *had* noticed a difference. The coming of Doctor Paul Quest seemed to be bringing out a lot of awareness today.

'Dell, did you tell Doctor Quest about Johnnie?'

He met the gaze in the mirror before turning away.

'No.'

'Oh, Dell, you *should* have. You know how Johnnie hates meeting anyone new. Why didn't you?'

'There was no reason to.'

Dell's voice was curt and she knew there was no point in arguing. He went through to their bathroom, turning on the taps. Sighing, Kate went slowly out of the room and down the stairs.

It was exactly seven o'clock when the front door bell rang. Kate went to open the door. Her recollection of Paul Quest had been reasonably accurate. A dark man with an easy manner and a friendly smile as he came into the hall.

'Have you had a good journey?'

'Not too bad, thanks. Far too much traffic, of course.'

Coming down the stairs, Dell thought what inanities people indulged in when they first met and decided, looking at Paul, that he had made the right choice for his new partner. This was a man who would make a good impression on patients, on people who, because they were ill, needed reassurance as well as medical treatment. Dell was relieved to find that his first impression of this man was now being renewed.

They were halfway through their first drinks when Lise came into the room. She was wearing a yellow dress which brought out the lights in her bright hair and Dell thought she looked particularly attractive and looked at Paul Quest to see his reactions but he could detect nothing in his manner except ordinary politeness as they continued to chat easily.

As the door opened a second time, Dell was conscious of Kate stiffening in her chair, of her eyes turning anxiously to Paul. Forestalling her, he made the introduction.

'This is our son, Johnnie.'

Johnnie, limping into the room, one shoulder crooked, thin hand outstretched, waited for the awkward, embarrassed pause which usually ensued. A pause usually accompanied by quickly averted eyes. But there was no pause, no change of expression as Paul, shaking his hand said, 'We've been discussing cars, mine in particular. I've just got a new one. Are you interested in them?'

Johnnie, taken completely by surprise, hesitated. His hand had been shaken firmly; he had immediately been accepted by this man as an ordinary human being, as if there was nothing wrong with him. For the first instant, he felt cheated. He was accustomed to making a definite impression; one that he could count on when he came into a room and he almost relished the readily predictable expressions he would see when he shook hands and people were careful not to press too hard in case they hurt his fingers. He felt like sulking. Enough to show this man that he thought him either heartless or unobservant. But he had no chance, he had to answer his question, and since he was intensely interested in cars, in no time, he was happily comparing various makes with someone who apparently regarded him as no different to anyone else in the room.

'When did you have Polio?'

The question fell into a sudden silence. A silence in which Kate's quickly indrawn breath was audible. Johnnie threw a quick glance in her direction.

'Just before I was three years old.'

Polio was a word never mentioned and nobody had ever been known to ask such a question. The experience was entirely novel and, curiously, Johnnie found he didn't mind.

Paul Quest seemed unaware of the sudden tension in the room as he looked the boy over with a smile.

'You're lucky to be so mobile.'

This too, was to Johnnie, an entirely new attitude to his shortcomings. Kate, always at his beck and call, took it upon herself to save him all effort, to anticipate his every need. It had, therefore, never entered Johnnie's head that he could do much more for himself if he cared to make the effort.

He said now, rather doubtfully, 'Well,

yes, I suppose I am.'

'Can you drive a car? Are you old enough?'

'Yes, I'm old enough, I'm just seventeen. I've tried driving Dad's up and down the drive, but that's all.'

Paul smiled at him.

'I'll teach you if you like. You can learn on mine.'

'Johnnie won't be able to drive.'

Kate's voice was icy and Paul turned to her, surprised.

'Why not?'

She stood up and started to walk towards the door.

'I would have thought that would have been obvious and — please Doctor Quest, don't start putting impossible ideas into Johnnie's head.'

She walked out of the room, closing the door behind her before Paul could reply and the next second, Dell had risen, saying quickly, 'I expect you'd like a wash before dinner. I think it's just about ready.'

Following him out, Paul came to the

conclusion that it would be best to drop the subject though he had the distinct impression that his partner was not in agreement with his wife.

For the rest of the evening, Kate's manner remained cool and everybody in the room with the apparent exception of Paul, was fully aware of the reason. Paul's conversation remained easy and it was evident that he had made a hit with Johnnie who scarcely took his eyes off him and maintained an unusual and animated interest in all the subjects touched upon.

When, eventually, Doctor Quest left, Johnnie went whistling cheerfully up to bed well satisfied with an evening which, for him, was different from any he had yet spent.

Downstairs, Dell waited for the criticism he knew would come. Kate commenced as soon as they were alone.

'I thought you said that he was a good doctor. What a way to behave with Johnnie. Too stupid — worse than stupid. What could he have been thinking about? You'll have to speak to him.'

Her words fell into silence and she turned to look at Dell. Surprised at the anger in his eyes, she said furiously, 'Are you trying to say that you don't agree with me?'

He turned away from her with a shrug.

'I've not said anything yet. Nor do I want to.'

He started to move towards the door but suddenly, she was standing in front of him.

'Surely, even you can't think it's a good thing for poor Johnnie to imagine he can drive a car. Think what it will mean to him when he finds he can't.'

'There's not much imagination about it. He can already handle a car. You heard him say, he often drives mine up and down the drive.'

'Yes. I heard. I had no idea that you had allowed him to do that. It was wrong of you. You know quite well that he could never drive on the road.'

'I know nothing of the kind and when the time comes, I've no doubt that he will be able to pass his test.'

Kate gazed at him in genuine bewilderment. It sounded like sheer madness. She made a helpless gesture with both hands.

'Oh, Dell — how *can* you? You know he can't do things like other people. It's cruel to let him think he can and then find it impossible.'

Her voice broke and Dell's eyes showed sudden pity. What was the use? They had been over this sort of thing so many times. She couldn't see that Johnnie should be given the chance to try and do things. She couldn't see that he needed a certain amount of independence. Her only wish was to protect him, to guard him for the rest of his life from any further ill which could befall him. Dell went to her now, putting his arm around her shoulders.

'Don't worry about it, darling. It will sort itself out.'

She twitched herself free of his arm.

'Oh, what's the use of talking? You simply don't understand. You never will.'

2

Inevitably, a few of the older patients insisted on seeing Dell; Dr. Manley had been their mainstay for so long, but within a month, the practice was working smoothly and Paul Quest becoming quite popular. One day, he went into Dell's consulting room.

'You know I promised Johnnie to teach him to drive my car?'

Dell looked up from his writing with a smile.

'Yes, I remember.'

Paul hitched himself on the edge of the desk.

'How do you feel about it?'

Dell said slowly, 'I am grateful for your interest. If you really mean't it, I'm sure Johnnie would be delighted.'

'I meant it but — well — it's a bit difficult.'

Dell put down his pen.

'You mean Kate's attitude.'

'Yes, I'm afraid I rather got off on the wrong foot there. I'm sorry about that and I wouldn't want to do anything further to upset her.'

For a moment, Dell sat staring at his desk, then he seemed to come to a decision.

'You'd better hear the story from the beginning. You'll understand better then. You see, when Johnnie was three, my wife took him with her to visit an aunt in Spain. Just before the end of the visit, Johnnie grew ill. The doctor was called and he said the boy had a severe attack of flu, which apparently was very prevalent there at that time. He gave her a prescription and said that he thought Johnnie would be fit to travel in thirty-six hours.'

Dell leaned forward, picked up his pen, took off the top then replaced it.

'Kate was unhappy about him and wanted to get him back home as quickly as possible so that I could deal with him.'

The top came off the pen again and Paul said, 'So Polio wasn't diagnosed until after you saw him?'

'No.'

After a moment Dell added, 'You see, Kate blames herself for that and for taking him to Spain in the first place. For weeks Johnnie was desperately ill and she literally wore herself out nursing him because he wanted her to be with him all the time. Finally, the whole nightmare became an obsession with her, an outsize guilt complex which she has never overcome. Her feeling is that the least she can do to make up to him is to devote the rest of her life to looking after him.'

Paul stood up.

'But Johnnie? What has this done to him?'

Dell shrugged.

'You can see that for yourself.'

Yes, Paul thought, he could see. The boy had a brilliant brain and the development of that Kate couldn't stop and Philip Cranston, as his tutor, had brought out the best in him. Johnnie was far above school standards in all subjects and he seemed to learn without special effort. It was on the physical side that Kate had done so much damage. Always with the best intentions, but nevertheless, untold damage. Paul wanted to ask his partner why he had allowed it to happen and as if aware of the coming question, Dell said, 'I should have fought what she was doing to him — ' he gestured and paused. 'It sounds like making excuses — perhaps it is — I had so little time and I was so desperately sorry for her and I knew that she was on the edge of a serious breakdown from the strain she was going through.' Again, a pause. 'Perhaps you find that difficult to understand, but even so, I didn't let this situation develop without a struggle.'

Paul said, 'No, I can see what you were up against.'

'You see,' Dell went on, 'Kate and I had always been so close, then, over Johnnie, whatever I suggested, we began to have rows. Something we'd never done before. She thought I just didn't understand — she still thinks so — she was so certain that the right thing, the only thing, was to wait on him, save him from doing anything for himself for the rest of his life. She hopes,' he ended quietly, 'that it will help to make up to him for — what he is.' After a moment's silence, he added, 'In the end, I regrettably and wrongly gave up the struggle.'

Paul said, 'It's not too late. A lot can still be done.'

'You think so?'

'I know so. This is something in which I have been particularly interested, something I have come into contact with.'

The older man looked eagerly at his partner. He had already discovered the tenacity of purpose in Paul's character and now, he was conscious of a small surge of hope.

He asked quietly, 'What do you think could be done?'

'On the physical side, very carefully graded exercises, and, quite as important, the psychological build up which he needs. Any idea of what he would like to do?'

Dell looked startled.

'No idea at all. The subject has never been broached. It has never been considered possible that he could ever do anything.'

'So that's something important to be found out.'

Suddenly, Dell smiled at him, feeling in that moment younger and more hopeful than he had for years.

'Did you mean — for *you* to find out?'

For a moment, Paul hesitated, then reperched himself on the desk.

'Well, it would depend if I had a free hand. I don't mean you, but Kate. I can't see her tolerating any interference from me. And, if she didn't — well — that would be that.'

Dell leaned forward, both hands on the desk.

'You really think you could help him?'

'Yes. I treated a much worse case than Johnnie's and it responded well. Only,' he hesitated, 'only, in that case, the boy had the will to fight.'

'And you don't think Johnnie has?'

'He hasn't been given the chance to know.'

There was a long silence before Dell said slowly, 'Would you be willing to give him that chance?'

'As long as my hands weren't tied — very willing.'

Dell stood up abruptly.

'Then there's only one way to do it. Kate mustn't know.'

'But wouldn't that create difficulties?'

'Yes. It would.'

Both men were silent for a minute, then Paul said, 'Look, before we decide anything, let me sound Johnnie out a bit and see what his reactions are.'

Without warning, the telephone rang shrilly and Dell picked up the receiver, saying as he did so, 'All right, I'll leave it to you and, I'm grateful.'

The call was for Paul and after he had left, Dell sat again at his desk, going over the possibilities of what had been said. Supposing Paul really could improve Johnnie's condition. What sort of future could there be for the boy? And Kate. What would she feel when she found out the — He had thought of the word deception, but surely what they proposed doing couldn't be classed as that? Something which was so wholly for the benefit of the boy?

There certainly would be difficulties, of that he was sure. Kate would be bitterly hurt. And angry. And for that, he would be deeply sorry. He always hated her to be hurt. She was so desperately vulnerable. Especially in connection with Johnnie.

For a second, he was tempted to call the whole thing off. But that had always been a fault. He had never had the courage of his own opinion where Johnnie was concerned, but now, the boy must come first, be the only consideration. He recollected the healthy little three-year-old that Johnnie had been until the polio had hit him. He thought of him as he was now. If there really was a chance for Johnnie, he must be given it, no matter what the cost.

Dell stood up with a sigh. It wouldn't be easy. So many things had changed with the coming of the new doctor, but this would be the greatest change of all. One which if successful, might alter all their lives. He thought with some bitterness as he picked up his bag, that the whole thing sounded too much like a fairy tale. Except for one thing. The peculiar trust he had in Paul. From what he now knew of him, he was convinced that this man would not hold out such hope unless he was certain that something, at least, was possible.

Paul, returning to the surgery just before five o'clock, walked through to the house to find Kate. She was in the garden and he went out to her.

'Johnnie finishes work at five, doesn't he?'

She looked at him speculatively.

'Yes, why?'

'Because I promised I would give him a chance to see how my car works.'

It was a long way round to saying he was going to give him a driving lesson. Kate frowned.

'And what does that mean, exactly?'

Paul smiled disarmingly.

'That if he likes to take a crack at driving it down the lane, he has my blessing.'

Kate tightened her mouth.

'I thought I made it plain when you first came that it would be quite impossible for Johnnie ever to drive.'

'But you didn't tell me why.'

'Isn't it obvious?'

'Not to me — no. Modern cars are extremely easy to handle and mine has an automatic gear which couldn't be simpler.'

She stood there in the sunlit garden, her expression stern, her mouth still tight, her lovely face drawn with tired lines, and suddenly, Paul was sorry for her, in that moment, all his irritation gone. He put one hand gently on her arm.

'Kate, please let me try to help him. He wants so much to do this. It would give him so much pleasure.'

She didn't pull away from his touch, and this, perhaps, was a small triumph in itself, for Paul knew that she had never forgiven him for that first night. After a moment, she moved.

'I suppose you will have to prove it to yourself before you see that I am right.'

Paul said quietly, 'Well, thank you for letting me try, anyway. I'll take good care of him,' and before she could change her mind, he turned back to the house in search of Johnnie who was putting his books away in the study where he worked.

'Any good?' he asked as if he didn't think it would be.

'Yes. Your mother says that I shall have to prove to myself that she is right and I am wrong,' Paul said gravely.

Johnnie made the sort of derisive sound any boy of his age might make to that kind of remark.

'I never thought she'd let us,' he said, including Paul in the need for permission.

With Johnnie in the driving seat, Paul thought that they had met defeat before they had started. Although the controls were light, Johnnie's fingers refused to operate the automatic gear lever. After a moment's struggle, his nerve went.

'I can't do it. It's no use. It's these stupid fingers. I can't do anything with them. I might have known,' he ended bitterly.

Paul sat calmly beside him. 'You give up very easily,' he said with calculated scorn and Johnnie flushed.

'I can't help it if my fingers are useless, can I?' His voice was petulant and half-ashamed.

'Your fingers are not useless. You manage to manipulate your father's car and — '

'This is different from Dad's.'

'Yes. It's easier, and the only reason you can't do it is because you are letting yourself panic. Everybody has to learn. Once you know how, there's nothing to it. Now, get on with it.'

At his third attempt, Johnnie triumphed and the car moved slowly down the drive. Neither of them spoke and the boy's hands were tight on the wheel, his face determined as they turned into the lane. Gradually, he relaxed and it was ten minutes later when they were in open country that Paul, looking at his watch, said mildly, 'I don't know how far you're thinking of going, but I have a surgery at six.'

With a grin, Johnnie slowed down, found a convenient place to turn and almost without effort, reversed the car and started on the return journey, bringing the car to a neat halt in the drive. For a moment, he sat back silently, pleasure apparent in his expression.

'I did it, didn't I?'

'Well, I told you you could. It didn't take you long to get the hang of it.'

Paul walked round to the driving side of the car, watching while Johnnie struggled awkwardly out and didn't offer to help him. Finally on his feet, he said with enthusiasm, 'That's one in the eye for Mum, isn't it?'

Whatever his own sentiments were, this wasn't the attitude Paul wanted from Johnnie. He turned on him sharply.

'Don't ever forget that your mother devotes her whole life to you and that everything she does is done for the best.'

He turned and walked quickly away without waiting to see the boy's suddenly shamefaced expression.

Kate was waiting, as Paul was sure she would be, just inside the surgery.

He said cheerfully, 'Well, we're back in one piece and I think he's enjoyed it.'

'You were gone a long time. I thought you were only going down the lane.'

Paul said lightly, 'I thought so too but

Johnnie had other ideas and I had to remind him that I had a surgery at six and he kindly consented to return.'

Kate looked at him in disbelief.

'You mean — *Johnnie* was driving all that time?'

Paul nodded.

'And enjoying every moment.'

Kate said angrily, 'The poor boy must be exhausted.'

'On the contrary, I think you will find him very relaxed and extremely pleased with himself.'

Without another word, she left him, to hurry back into the house. Doubtless, he thought unkindly, to condole with Johnnie over the rough treatment he had received.

3

Paul threw himself on the grass beside Johnnie and Johnnie said, 'This is an unlikely time for you to be here, isn't it?'

'Yes, I'm waiting for Dell. We have to see a case together.'

Johnnie regarded him wistfully.

'You like being a doctor, don't you?'

Paul nodded. 'Yes. What do you want to do?'

Johnnie said scornfully, 'How could *I* do anything?'

'Why not?'

Johnnie sat up angrily. 'With a weak back, a crooked shoulder, a limp — and silly hands? You must be daft.'

'But you're not imbecile. I'm told you have an excellent brain and know how to use it.'

'But you know *why* I can't do anything.' Johnnie's voice was petulant.

'I know you *don't* do anything. I certainly don't know that you can't. And nor do you.' His voice was quietly scathing and it got the reception he expected. The boy scrambled up to stand in front of him.

'Look at me,' he demanded dramatically. 'What good would I be for anything like this?'

Paul's eyes roved appraisingly over him.

'One leg slightly shorter than the other,' he assessed brutally. 'One back not as strong as most, one crooked shoulder. One exceptionally good brain already proved capable of passing any necessary exams.' He paused. 'I'm not suggesting that you take up a navvy's job.'

Johnnie was too astonished to do anything but whip up his anger further.

'I think your joke is in very poor taste.'

He was striving for dignity but his voice shook. Paul nodded.

'Oh, I agree. If it *were* a joke. As it

happens, I'm serious.'

Johnnie sat down again in his clumsy way. There was a long silence which Paul made no effort to break. At last, Johnnie asked, 'Then, what did you mean?'

'Well, let's tackle this on a practical level. Ruling out the more strenuous things, given a choice, what would you most like to do?'

As Johnnie stared at him, Paul watched the expressions flitting across his face. Disbelief; confusion; slight hope, and finally, something which hurt Paul to see and which made him think suddenly of a dog which has been ill-treated and who had suddenly found a friend.

After a long moment, Johnnie said incredulously, 'You really believe I could, don't you?'

'Certainly. Why not? There are plenty of things to choose from. Think of some.'

Suddenly, Johnnie smiled.

'I don't need to think. I know what I

would *like* to do more than anything else, only — ' he paused, then added flatly, 'only I don't suppose I could.'

'Oh, for God's sake don't start taking that defeatist attitude. You'll never get anywhere like that. Now then, what is it?'

Johnnie said shyly, 'I've always wanted to write plays.'

Paul raised his eyebrows.

'Then why the hell don't you get on with it?'

'But — but how could I? I can't even hold a pen properly.'

'How do you prepare your work for Philip?'

'Type it with two fingers.'

'Then, what are you waiting for?' Paul's voice was scathing and Johnnie flushed.

'Yes, but — '

'But what?'

'Well, I mean, I don't see how I could. I — '

'The only reason you don't see how you could is because you never think or do anything for yourself. Your mother waits on you hand and foot and encourages you to be thoughtless and lazy and to think of yourself as helpless. You are ready to accept that as the ultimate for you.' Paul paused, his voice hard. 'In other words, it remains with you to decide if you ever intend to get away from that pattern, or whether you are prepared to go on accepting your mother's sacrifice for the rest of your life.' He drew a deep breath. 'If you see yourself as an invalid, you will remain one. On the other hand, as long as you are prepared to accept certain limitations, you can lead a normal life and do what you want to do.'

Paul stopped, then added slowly, 'But you have to believe you can do it. Nobody can do that for you.'

Paul watched Kate cross the lawn with a small tray in her hands. She placed it carefully on the table beside Johnnie, asking him anxiously if he could reach it and if he was warm enough. Would he like her to bring him out a sweater?

He answered her irritably, very conscious of Paul. Kate offered Paul some coffee but he told her he was just leaving. When she had gone, he looked coldly at Johnnie.

'There,' he said scornfully, 'you have a very good example of what I have been saying.'

Johnnie looked up sullenly.

'I don't know what you mean.'

'Then that makes it all the worse.'

Johnnie shrugged.

'What are you talking about?'

'I'll tell you. That was a good example of what you *could* have done, but didn't. You sat and watched your mother carry that tray all the way from the house and you never moved a muscle.'

Paul watched colour flood into the boy's face as he said rudely, 'Oh — be your age. You know perfectly well that I'd only have dropped it. Besides — she always brings it. She always has.'

Paul said bitterly, 'And she always will unless *you* stop her. And that's your only hope.' He began to turn away and Johnnie said desperately, 'You *know* I can't hold things in my hands.'

Paul turned to look at him.

'Except a steering wheel. But then, you *wanted* to do that.'

Without giving Johnnie a chance to answer, he walked across the lawn, down the drive and into the surgery.

Johnnie watched the retreating figure. Just how angry can a back look, he wondered? Quite suddenly, he felt ashamed. He *had* mastered the car because it was something he wanted to do. Paul was right there. He thought of his mother. But she *liked* bringing him coffee and until this morning, he had accepted it without thought. But this morning, he had hated Paul seeing her do it. That, he reminded himself, had been because Paul had been so scathing. Really, the whole conversation had been absurd. Hadn't it?

He leaned back in his chair, holding his coffee cup with both hands while he sipped. Why should Paul trouble to say any of those things unless he really believed them? It wouldn't be like him. A Play? Could he ever write a Play? He was always thinking up ideas, always reading other people's Plays but it had never occurred to him that he himself could ever write one. Suddenly, he was possessed with an entirely new sensation and after a minute, he recognised it as hope. The feeling was small and frail, a breath of disaster would blow it away, but it was there and he hung on to it, lying in his chair with his eyes shut and the coffee cup still held in mid air.

'Darling — do you feel all right?'

He hadn't heard her cross the lawn and he sat up abruptly, spilling some of the coffee. He looked at her almost with dislike.

'Of course I feel all right. Why shouldn't I?'

Kate glanced at him in swift surprise.

'I only thought — ' she began and he interrupted her roughly.

'Well don't. You're always fussing me. Why can't you leave me alone?'

Kate stared at him, suddenly disastrously near tears. He had never spoken to her like this. What could be wrong? Perhaps he was ill. Blinking back her tears, she prepared to be tactful.

'All right then, if you've finished your coffee, I'll take your cup.'

'I haven't finished yet and — you needn't come back for it, I'll bring it in myself.'

She stared again incredulously. What had come over him?

'But darling, you can't — '

'I said, don't fuss. I've told you, *I'll* bring it in.'

For a moment, she stood looking at the scowling face, then turned and went back to the house.

He finished the coffee, regretting his rudeness then struggled up out of the chair still holding the cup. Because he was off balance, he nearly fell and he grasped hold of the table to right himself and set the cup on its saucer. He picked up the tray with both hands and started off across the lawn and because he was quite unaccustomed to carrying anything, he stumbled along until he reached the step to the back door. Carefully negotiating it, he was conscious of his mother watching through the window. Keeping his eyes on the tray, he took it over to the sink. He tried to turn on the tap but it was stiff and he had to use both hands. Behind him, Kate watched silently but he knew well enough what she was thinking; knew that she was resisting the temptation to come to his aid because of what he had said in the garden.

Suddenly the tap turned and nearly boiling water gushed out over his wrists and in spite of himself, he cried out with the pain.

'Oh, darling, what *have* you done. Let me look.'

Savagely, he pushed her away and started to pick up the cup in the sink, but suddenly his fingers were useless and as he dropped it, it broke in the sink. He looked at it with a kind of dumb hatred.

'Oh, Johnnie dear. It doesn't matter. It was only an old one. Let me look at your poor hands.'

For Johnnie, her sympathy was the last straw and he stumbled blindly out of the kitchen and up to his room. He heard Kate start to follow him and before she could reach the landing, he shut and locked the door.

For a few minutes, he stood leaning against it, conscious that he was trembling. Then he threw himself down on the bed. He pressed his fingers against his eyes to keep back the shaming tears from spilling out.

So that is the end of that, he thought angrily, hating Paul, hating himself. The end of Paul's stupid hopes, of all the rubbish he had talked about. He might have known — he *had* known he wouldn't be able to do anything. His mother had been right all the time. He'd proved it, hadn't he? Just now, with that ruddy cup. Proved how useless Paul's ideas were. Suddenly he wondered what Paul would say when he heard what a fiasco he had made of his first efforts at independence.

Kate tried the door, then knocked.

'Let me in darling.'

Her voice held a hint of comfort. At first, he resisted it, not answering, then, the thought of her waiting outside was too much for him and he got off the bed and opened the door, returning to the bed as she entered the room.

'I'm sorry I was rude to you mother,' he forced himself to say without looking at her and for answer, she sat down on the bed and took his hand.

'It's all right darling. I don't know what came over you but it's over now, so don't think about it any more. Just lie quietly here and rest.'

Johnnie accepted that silently but he knew as she said it that it wasn't over. He was thinking about Paul, in his mind's eye, the scorn there would be in his face when he was told.

He closed his eyes, not listening to what Kate was saying. If he couldn't face that scorn, what was the alternative? It didn't bear thinking about because it meant that he would have to try again. He didn't want to. What was the use? All he wanted was to go back to before Paul came. It had been peaceful then. Then came the thought that he hadn't been able to drive a car. That was something, wasn't it?

He lay with his eyes closed, hoping that his mother would think he was asleep and go away. When finally she did, he continued to lie there, feeling that he had reached the lowest ebb of despair. His greatest wish was that Paul should not hear of his stupid failure but knew that his mother would not be able to resist telling him.

The next morning, reading history in the garden, he listened for the sound of Paul's car. If he could get through today without seeing him, perhaps it would be all right, but looking up from his book, he saw Paul crossing the lawn towards him.

'Congratulations.'

Johnnie's expression was sullen and

he wouldn't meet Paul's eyes.

'On what?'

'On a quick start.'

'I don't know what you're talking about.'

'Don't you? Then you must be a lot dimmer than I thought.'

Carefully, Johnnie put down the book because his hands were shaking too much to hold it.

'You needn't trouble to be sarcastic.'

Paul lowered himself on to the grass.

'Sarcastic? Oh, no, I could do a great deal better than that if I wanted to be sarcastic. Can't you understand that I literally wanted to congratulate you on a really good effort?'

For the first time, Johnnie looked at him and the obvious sincerity of his expression surprised him.

'A *good* effort! You must be crazy. It was a disaster, and not one I am likely to repeat. I don't know why I listened to such rubbish in the first place.' He paused. 'Why did she have to tell you, anyway?'

'Effort doesn't necessarily have to end in success to be classed as good. And she told me because everything you do is of immense importance to her.' He gave Johnnie a sly grin. 'Added to which, such an unexpected exploit on your part has left her with the impression that you must be sickening for something.'

In spite of himself, Johnnie smiled but he said gruffly, 'Anyway, it's cured me of being stupid and I'm not likely to try again.'

Paul heaved himself up from the grass and stood for a moment looking down at the boy.

'No. Your tactics will be different this morning. Today you'll go in and fetch your own coffee.'

Without waiting for an answer, he walked quickly away to the house.

Johnnie stared after him angrily. Like hell he would. He'd no intention of making a fool of himself a second time. He'd finished with daydreams. Picking up his book, he began to read. Yesterday, he had found the book absorbing; today, it could not hold his attention and he kept looking at his watch.

At five minutes to eleven, he strolled into the kitchen where, as he knew she would be, Kate was making the coffee. She looked up brightly.

'I was just going to bring it out to you.'

'I'll take it.'

He tried to sound nonchalant but Kate gave him a sharp glance.

'It's all right darling, I'll do it.'

'No.'

Johnnie was surprised at the vehemence of his own voice. He stepped forward to take the tray from her. For one instant he was tempted to put it down on the table and drink the coffee there, but that would be compromise. He turned slowly, carrying it out of the kitchen and across the lawn. It seemed a long walk to the little table by his chair. When finally he put it down, he spilled a few drops of the coffee into the saucer.

4

Kate lay flat in the bed, waiting for Dell to come back from the bathroom. She knew the various stages of his toilet from the thorough brushing of teeth to the final brushing of hair, and she could tell when this stage had been reached because he always whistled. Now, he stopped and the next minute the bathroom door opened and he came into the room, kicking off his slippers as he turned to look at her as he reached the bed. Smiling, he bent to kiss her.

'You know something? Your hair's still as bright as the day I married you.'

She met his gaze without smiling. He had always said things like that to her. Small, disconcertingly observant things which showed her suddenly that he still really *saw* her. Sometimes she was glad, but tonight she had something else on her mind. Something which had to be said.

Dell put out the light and settled himself beside her. His arm stretched across her and began to pull her round towards him. Slowly and carefully she removed it.

'No, Dell. I have to talk to you.'

'Now?'

'Yes, now. We seem to be so seldom alone that this is the only time.'

Sighing, he waited, thinking he knew what was coming. What he didn't know was how he was going to deal with it. He thought she would start as she usually did by saying, 'I'm worried about Johnnie.' But she didn't. Instead, she said, 'How valuable is Paul to you?'

He imagined he must have misheard her and started to repeat it. 'How valuable — '

'Yes. What I mean is, could you replace him?'

Dell turned on to his back and put his hands behind his head. This was certainly different from what he had expected. A new approach entirely, yet instinctively, he knew this would lead to Johnnie. He answered cautiously.

'I've certainly no wish to do anything of the kind. Why should I? He is an excellent doctor and a great help to me.'

'I suppose you can't see the tremendous influence he is gaining over Johnnie. The poor boy's quite changed since he came and it's entirely due to Paul. Surely you must have noticed?'

Oh yes, he had noticed; noticed with gratitude the improvement both mentally and physically in his son. But he also knew what she was driving at. Knew and understood what this was doing to her. He didn't need to be a doctor to realise what a blow this must be to Kate whose every thought and aim had been to live for and serve a boy whom she believed to be helpless. Every day Johnnie was becoming more and more independent in the small things which she had always done for him. It must be constantly borne in on her that she was becoming less necessary to him. And that must hurt. The small things would become larger ones until finally he would be able to do without her altogether. The whole meaning of her life would be gone and he knew that subconsciously, this was her fear. Yet, wasn't that the equivalent to saying that she didn't want him to get any better?

If he said that to her, she would be horrified but love and fear are not reasonable emotions and it was from these she was suffering now. Yes, and jealousy.

He said, 'There is certainly no change for the worse in Johnnie. You surely can't think that?'

'Oh, Dell — can't you see? All the time he tries to do more than he is able, then something goes wrong. He drops or breaks something, and then he is worried. Can't you see how bad that is for him? It makes him bad-tempered and restless.'

He said gently, 'Don't you want him to be more independent? To be able to

53

do things for himself like other boys?'

There was an appreciable silence before she answered.

'Yes, of course I do.' She paused. 'But only if he is able to do things properly — easily and without it worrying him but Paul — forcing him isn't right. He never tried to do any of these things before Paul came.'

If he were brutal enough, he could tell her that that was because she had never let him try. But that had always been his trouble. With Kate, he had always been weak, always hated to hurt her. When Johnnie was so ill and they'd thought they were going to lose him, he had given way all along the line because he had been afraid of a complete breakdown for her. He thought now, that he had been just as much at fault over the boy as she had. More, because he was a doctor and had known from the beginning that her method was wrong.

He answered her slowly, knowing before he started that nothing he could say would satisfy her.

'You must believe me when I say that Paul has done nothing in any way to force Johnnie.'

'He forced him to drive his car. Johnnie would never have thought of it if Paul hadn't told him he would teach him.'

'Darling, I told you that Johnnie had been whizzing my car up and down the drive for some time and Paul's is much easier to handle than mine because of its automatic gears. Why should it be bad for him to be able to drive? It was something he wanted to do.'

She said, coming out into the open, 'But it's so dangerous.'

'No more dangerous for him than for you or me. Paul says he is a good and careful driver who doesn't take undue risks.'

Kate said sharply, 'He is with Paul a great deal too much. He is far too much under his influence.'

And away from yours, Dell thought unkindy.

He said, 'You've never liked him, have you?'

'No. That first night — look at the way he behaved and, he's arrogant, self-opinionated and far too sure of himself.'

'I don't think you're being fair to him. I've never found him arrogant in the practice and I'm quite sure no patient has either or I should have heard about it. Patients seem to like him.'

'Then, you won't get rid of him?'

'Get *rid* of him — no — certainly not. How could I? On what grounds?'

After a long silence, Kate said, 'Incompatability, or something of that sort?'

In the darkness, Dell smiled.

'That's usually for divorce, I fancy. Besides, we get on extremely well and he works remarkably hard and I am grateful to him for taking so much off my shoulders.'

Kate sighed.

'Then, if you won't do that, will you

speak to him about Johnnie, tell him not to interfere with him? Tell him you won't have it.'

He put out his hand to touch and press her shoulder.

'Kate, I promise you that if Paul ever does anything but good to Johnnie I will tell him, but so far, he *has* done nothing but good. You must trust me in this, darling. I know what I am doing.'

She turned swiftly away from him saying bitterly, 'Oh, what's the use? I might have known it wasn't any good asking you. You've never understood about Johnnie. You've never wanted to.'

He didn't answer her. That wouldn't do any good either, but he continued to lie awake with his mind tugging him both ways.

He knew that Kate's way was not right, but what about his own? Guilty in the first place for his weakness and now, when he was trying to rectify his mistakes, wasn't he going about it the wrong way? The easy way? Using someone else to carry it out. Aiding and abetting that someone in deceiving poor Kate?

He moved restlessly in the bed and felt her shift away as if she needed to be as far from him as possible.

He didn't like that word deceiving, yet that is what they were doing, with Johnnie himself included in the deception. Should he tell her now that Paul was treating the boy, and with very encouraging results? He tried some phrases out in his mind, but none was adequate to combat the violent reaction it would receive from her. Dell knew that whatever he said, whatever proof he offered, Kate wouldn't listen. Her mind was already made up about Johnnie. She was the only person who understood his needs. She was the only person who could supply them and her mind was determinedly dead to any other suggestion ... Everything else *must* be wrong. Not normally a stupid woman, she was unassailable when it came to Johnnie; a brick wall which would not shift an inch.

Dell found it impossible to sleep and he thought that Kate too, was awake. He longed to touch her, to comfort and love her, but he knew what her reaction would be and left her alone. Eventually, he slept from sheer exhaustion, but nothing was solved. Everything was just the same as it had been.

5

While lying awake, Kate, with some anger, came to a definite conclusion. There was next to no hope that she could persuade Dell to change his partner and she admitted to herself that she had been wrong and stupid to suggest it. It was obvious too, that Dell didn't intend doing anything to stop Paul interfering with Johnnie. There was only one thing left and she must do it herself. To this end, she waited for Paul outside the surgery the next morning.

She said coldly, 'I should be glad if you can spare me a few minutes before you go out. It is necessary that I talk to you.'

Paul, giving her a quick glance, followed her into the house. When they reached the morning-room, she didn't offer him a chair but he pulled one out for her and, reluctantly, she took it. Paul sat down in one facing her, crossing his legs and looking completely relaxed. Kate began a trifle nervously.

'It's about Johnnie — as I expect you know.'

'It doesn't exactly surprise me. What have you in mind?'

'I should be grateful if you will leave him alone. You are making him do too much and, I don't like all this driving.'

'What makes you think he is doing too much?'

Kate said emphatically, 'He must not be forced to do things beyond his strength. He has to rest.'

'Why?'

She looked at him in genuine amazement.

'You're a doctor, and you ask me that?'

'Perhaps I say it *because* I'm a doctor. It is certainly high time somebody asked it.'

He gestured towards the chair from which she had started to rise.

'No. Let's try to discuss this rationally, shall we?'

Surprisingly, Kate found herself sitting down again but she said angrily, 'I don't know what you mean by that, but I think your behaviour most extraordinary.'

'I'm sorry you should feel that, but you have never liked me, have you? From the very first night when I asked Johnnie when he had had Polio. You see, I didn't know that in this house Polio was a dirty word never to be mentioned.'

'Do you really imagine the poor boy *wants* to be reminded of it?'

He shook his head.

'No, *I* don't, but apparently *you* do.'

Kate glanced at him warily, suddenly feeling that she was losing the initiative.

'I don't know what you can possibly mean.'

'Well, isn't treating him as an invalid, making him feel entirely useless and unable in any way to lead a normal existence, forcing him to be aware of it every minute of his life?'

Kate stared indignantly, wondering how this comparative stranger dared to speak to her in this way of her own son. Yet she reluctantly recognised the sincerity coming through with the arrogance. She struggled against even the remote possibility that his words might have sense or meaning. She was very much aware that this rather odd conversation was not shaping in any way as she had planned.

She said at last, 'You don't seem to understand how delicate he is. His energies have to be carefully conserved.'

'Did somebody tell you that, or is it your own idea?' His tone was dry and, she thought, contemptuous and for some reason, she stumbled over her reply.

'I — I would have thought that was obvious. You only need to look at him.'

'He has never been given a chance to develop his strength; never been given any independence to prove himself. You have always treated him as an invalid and so, he has become one. It is as simple as that.'

Kate said icily, 'And I suppose you have an instant remedy for all these mistakes I have made with my son. I suppose you are capable of making him into a Hercules overnight.'

Paul smiled.

'No. Nothing instant, I'm afraid, but for the last six or seven weeks we have been carrying out a series of very carefully graded exercises which have caused a marked improvement in his muscles.'

Kate began to feel her heart pound as she stared at him unbelievingly.

'You've been doing this? Do you mean to tell me that you have been carrying out these exercises on my son without consulting me? Without my permission?'

'But not without Dell's.'

His voice was very quiet and for a moment, Kate digested this bitter knowledge silently. How could Dell do this to her? Perhaps it wasn't true.

'You are telling me that my husband is in agreement with this crazy treatment?'

'Yes. He is in complete agreement. I should certainly not have undertaken it otherwise.'

'Why wasn't I consulted?'

Even as she spoke, Kate knew the answer to that.

'I suppose it was your idea to treat him behind my back.'

Her voice was hard and bitter.

Paul sidestepped that by telling her that the intention had been to prove his theory before telling her.

'And why was that necessary?'

Paul watched her angry expression.

'Would you have agreed to it in the first place?'

Kate moved irritably.

'Of course not. I would never have dreamed of allowing you to have interfered with him in this way.'

'Then — there is your answer.'

Kate sat with her hands tightly clasped in her lap. This must be stopped at once.

Paul said, 'Can you tell me honestly that Johnnie has in any way been less well during the last weeks?'

Her eyes flicked up at him, then away as she suddenly recollected that more than once she had thought with pleasure how well Johnnie was looking. His face had lost its usual pinched look.

She said sullenly, 'He is trying to do too much. It must be a strain on him.'

'He is doing a little more each day. Just as much as he himself wants to do. No one is forcing him; he is just finding pleasure in being *able* to do things he hasn't done before.'

He watched the struggle going on in Kate's very expressive face. She so much wanted to believe herself right, to believe that only she knew what was good for Johnnie. She resented bitterly that anyone else should be able to help him. Suddenly, he was sorry for her and said gently, 'I realise how hard this must be for you. You have devoted your life to Johnnie and I know that everything you have done you have done for the best, but there is such a thing as getting too close to your subject to be able to see straight and now Johnnie needs to be given the chance to have a life of his own.'

Kate lifted her hands in a wide gesture.

'But, his lameness, his poor back, his hands. What can he do? He's so helpless.'

'He is only helpless because you have made him so.'

She left her chair abruptly and went over to the window, standing there silently. At last, she turned.

'Why are you doing this? Why should it mean anything to you? I suppose it is just a medical challenge. Just an experiment for which you are using Johnnie.'

He looked at her coldly.

'I fancy you are asking me if Johnnie is merely a rat in a laboratory.'

Because he saw her flinch, he regretted the words as soon as they were spoken. Kate said quietly, 'Perhaps that is just what he is to you and if your experiment is unsuccessful, Johnnie will have to be put back in his cage and be worse off than before.'

'Why, worse off?'

'Because you will have raised his hopes and let him think he can achieve the impossible.'

Paul left his chair, going to stand by the mantelpiece. He picked up a small carved box then put it down again very carefully. They had come too far to finish like this and suddenly he felt compelled to explain to this woman who hated him because she felt that he was taking her son away from her. Perhaps he owed her an explanation.

'When I first came, I was angry to think so much time had been wasted.'

Kate turned towards him as he began to speak.

'I was angry because nobody seemed aware of the boy's potentials. He has a brilliant brain but it didn't occur to anybody that he could *do* anything or *be* anything.' He paused trying to clarify his thoughts. 'You were right in thinking I regarded him as a medical challenge. I did; I still do, but there's a lot more to it than that.' He waved a hand towards the chairs they had left. 'Let's sit down, shall we?'

Kate sat reluctantly, but he felt she was at least willing to listen.

'I have a brother who is much younger than I and soon after I qualified, he developed Polio.'

He saw Kate's quick movement and was conscious of her watching him closely.

'His attack must have been more severe than Johnnie's for he was scarcely mobile at all. But he was a fighter, and so was my mother. From the first, Charles was determined to beat it.'

Kate said quickly, 'And you helped him?'

He nodded.

'We all three worked together. I studied all the newest and best methods of treatment and eventually, we got him on his feet again. With braces. It's the most he will ever be able to do. One hand is still pretty well useless, but with the other, he can do most things.'

'But how can he ever — '

Paul smiled at her.

'Ever *do* anything? Well — he hasn't the same chance as Johnnie, firstly because he is not as mobile and secondly, he hasn't Johnnie's brilliant brain, but Charles is artistic and he is learning to paint. I have one of his pictures in my flat. I'd like you to see it.'

There was a long silence during which Paul wondered if it had been worth while telling her.

Kate said, 'I'm sorry about your brother and — thank you for telling me. Have you told Johnnie this?'

'No. Nor Dell, but I thought it might help you to understand what I felt about Johnnie when I first came.' Suddenly, he smiled. 'Johnnie's a charmer, I've become very fond of him.'

He could almost follow the thoughts in Kate's mind as she sat silently, thinking of what he had said. The battle was by no means won but he thought that things might be on a more reasonable level from now on. Finally, he said, 'So you see, I have a fair knowledge of what I am doing — and why I am doing it.'

When she didn't answer, he asked, 'Have I your blessing now?'

Kate put her hand up to her head in a worried gesture.

'I — I don't know. You've confused me. It can't be wrong to want to protect Johnnie when — '

'Perhaps not. In some ways. But they have to be the right ones. As Johnnie becomes more independent, he will learn to protect himself inasmuch as he will know and accept his own limitations but the work he is choosing should be well within those limits.'

'*Work* he is choosing?'

'Johnnie wants to write plays.'

'*Plays?* Johnnie?'

'Yes. Why not? With his brain and his intense wish to do so, he should be able to write good ones.'

Paul looked at his watch and stood up.

'I'm late, I must go.'

He stood up, uncharacteristically hesitant, saying finally, 'I hope we understand each other a little better now.'

Kate made her mouth into a tight line.

'At least you have given me a lot to think about.'

As Paul went out to his car, he reflected that at best, it could be called a reluctant truce, and with that, for the moment, he had to be content.

6

After Paul left, Kate remained where she was. She sat very still. At first not thinking at all, just letting her brain listen inattentively to the sound of the electric cleaner overhead. And when that stopped, she listened to a blackbird singing outside the open french window. For a while, her mind remained pitifully empty, rather as if the electric cleaner had sucked everything out of it. It was quite pleasant, in a way; peaceful and she didn't have to make any effort.

She heard Mrs. Matthews come downstairs, banging the cleaner against each one as she came. Mrs. Matthews would be wondering, Kate thought, what she was doing sitting about in the middle of the morning, but there would be coffee quite soon. That would be nice too. She found that her head was aching and she pushed back her heavy hair.

If Doctor Paul Quest hadn't come to the practice, none of this would have happened. They would all have been abe to continue doing the things they had always done, quietly and without any interference. She could have gone on looking after Johnnie. Not now. Not any more.

'Aren't you well, then?'

Mrs. Matthews advanced into the room, bearing a cup and saucer in her hand.

'Oh, thank you — just a bit of a headache, that's all.'

'Well then, you sit there and drink that. Coffee's good for a headache.'

Kate smiled gratefully as she took the cup from her.

'You stay there then. I'm going to do me silver in a minute.'

The room was very quiet after Mrs. Matthews had left and the blackbird had stopped singing.

Stirring the coffee, Kate thought in a detached way that it was odd that you

74

could live with someone you loved for so many years and know so little about them. She had always thought of Dell as entirely predictable, thought she knew and understood most things about him and how he would react to any given set of circumstances.

She had been wrong, of course; all these years, she had been wrong. He had been perfectly willing to deceive her at the first whim of a stranger.

Kate sat up, put down the coffee cup. No. That was hardly fair. Although she couldn't get away from the deceit, she allowed that at least his intentions must have been good. Good, but dangerously mistaken and against everything she could wish.

And Johnnie? Johnnie must have been in it too. Yes, of course. He was the central figure; the whole cause and reason of the experiment.

She picked up the cup, holding it with both hands and sipping slowly. Mrs. Matthews made good coffee. She was enjoying it.

So, it was plain that Johnnie must want to get away from her too. She let the thought run over the surface of her mind, a sort of unreal experiment which she needn't repeat if she didn't want to. But Johnnie only wanted this because he had been persuaded into it by dangling impossible prizes in front of him. She could make him change his mind, for surely her influence must be greater than Paul's. Than Dell's? She frowned. Dell had never gone against her before, never suggested any course of action to the boy which didn't fall in with her own wishes. Perhaps it wouldn't be so easy to make Johnnie give up what he was doing; she couldn't be sure.

Dell had always let her have her way but he had never approved of it. Did that account for his attitude now?

Setting down the empty cup, Kate began to think more clearly. Was Lise in this too? If so, then she herself was playing a lone hand. The thought suddenly frightened her. She needed help, she needed the backing of her own family. Her hands holding tightly to the arms of the chair, she admitted to herself that never before had she thought in these terms. Until now, everything she had done for Johnnie had been done with a loving compulsion. It had always seemed natural and right. She recollected unwillingly that Dell had once referred to it as an obsession. Which was nonsense.

Sunlight touched her through the open window and suddenly she felt she needed to be in the air. Standing for a moment just outside, she held up her face to the sun, conscious of the comfort of its heat ... She needed comfort just now but where would she find it? If they were all against her, she would have to fight alone.

Kate walked slowly across the lawn, only half aware of the flower scents around her. Was she going to fight? Fight to keep her place with Johnnie, fight to hold him to her? How could that be wrong? He was her son and he still needed her. Nothing could convince her against that.

At midday Mrs. Matthews came to tell her that she was leaving.

'I see you're better,' she said cheerfully. 'I told you the coffee'd do you good.'

After a little while, Kate went into the house to prepare lunch. As she passed the study door she could hear the murmur of voices as Johnnie and Philip worked.

At lunch, she had the sensation that she was standing outside herself, judging these characters as if they were strangers. Dell, although he rushed in late, was beginning to eat his meals in a less hurried manner. Johnnie, though still with a small appetite, now seemed to enjoy what he ate and, Kate noticed with her new, detached manner, he seemed to be holding his knife and fork more easily and firmly and there was a fraction of colour in his thin cheeks.

Lise, she thought, seemed preoccupied and wondered if it was to do with

Philip who himself was doing justice to the meal. He stayed for lunch three times a week and worked on with Johnnie in the afternoons. Kate regarded him with approval. He would make a pleasant son-in-law. One with whom she could get on very easily. She wondered why Lise was taking so long to make up her mind. Perhaps after all, she was not in love with him.

Kate had hoped to be able to talk to Dell before he went out again but with an early appointment, he left immediately after lunch.

In the garden, she commenced weeding the long border. Gardening always soothed her and she made a conscious effort to put her problem out of her mind. Working to a rhythm, she loosened the weeds, shook off the earth and placed them in the trug beside her. But before long, the rhythm broke and she sat back on her heels gazing down at the newly disturbed earth. She still felt as if she were outside herself, as if her mind were detached from her body.

The sensation provided a very necessary cushion to the intensity of her feelings, but it wouldn't last and she would have to face what was happening, and for this, she would need all her strength, all her powers of persuasion to stop what they were doing to Johnnie. It didn't occur to her that Johnnie himself might be developing ideas about his independence. She thought only in terms of his exploitation and of herself as his avenging angel.

She recollected early fights between herself and Dell; fights which she nearly always won without too much trouble. This time, it would be different and for one terrifying moment, she wondered whether her strength would be equal to the struggle. But she must win or there would be nothing left for her. Her life would be completely empty and meaningless. Because she had allowed herself to envisage defeat, she began to dread the encounter she must have with Dell.

Yet, when it came, there was no

angry shouting and very little argument. You can't argue with a stone wall, and that is what Dell seemed to have become. Kate had expected and dreaded the difficulties but she hadn't thought it would be impossible from the start.

She looked at Dell in dismay. This man was a stranger. He was not only the man who had deceived her, but he was showing an implacability of which she would not have thought him capable. She had always known and traded on the fact that he hated to hurt her and had based all their previous arguments on this one known fact. Today, it availed her nothing. Not only that, but he was accusing her of selfishness.

'Can't you see that it is only because you *want* to go on waiting on him that you are refusing to admit that already he is showing improvement?'

To Kate, they were cruel words and unjust. How could it be selfish to want to help Johnnie?

As if he understood what was in her

mind, Dell said, 'Why won't you admit that Johnnie's able to do more and that it is doing him good?'

For answer, she turned on him.

'Don't you realise what Paul is doing? I suppose he didn't tell you about his brother?'

She saw Dell's startled glance and took advantage of it.

'No. I see that he didn't. His younger brother developed Polio soon after Paul qualified and he — ' she hesitated. When Paul had told her, she had felt sympathy, had accepted and admired what he had done for his brother, but now, she was preparing to use it as a weapon against him.

'He insisted on giving the boy exercises and heaven knows what else.'

Dell looked at her coldly.

'With what result?'

For a moment, Kate hesitated and she couldn't meet his eyes as she said slowly, 'He can't walk without sticks . . . ' She threw out her hands in a desperate gesture. 'Oh, can't you see — Paul was experimenting with his own brother and now he's experimenting with Johnnie. You can't allow it, you must stop him before he does any damage.'

As Dell watched her, he underwent a revulsion of feeling. His usual sense of pity for her was entirely missing. It was as if Paul's initial action had given him the strength to do what he should have done all along. Nothing, not even Kate, was going to deflect him from what they were doing for Johnnie. They were on the right course and they were going to stay there. It remained for him to make this clear to her. For this, he would need all his courage.

They were standing at the wooded end of the garden in the fading evening light and the low sun still reached them through the trees. To him, she looked lovely in her angry, tragic concern but he hardened his heart, speaking clearly and slowly.

'I think you know that you are being less than fair to Paul and that he was not experimenting on his brother and neither is he on Johnnie. He has, doubtless because of his brother — specialised in this subject and knows a lot about it. He is extremely cautious and is taking things very slowly and although I know you are determined not to admit it, you must know in your own mind that Johnnie is better in every way since Paul came.'

'Since Paul came,' she repeated bitterly. 'I wish Paul had never come. We were happy until he started to change everything. Can't you see? He's so damned sure of himself — he's even changed you.'

'Changed *me*?' Dell's surprise was genuine.

'Yes, you would never have deceived me if it hadn't been for Paul.'

In its way, it was true, because none of this *would* be happening but for Paul but Dell said firmly, 'It was I who decided not to tell you until we saw the results of the exercises.'

'Oh, Dell — how *could* you?'

He said ruthlessly, 'Would you have agreed?'

'Of course not.'

'No. This was something I *had* to do. I had to give Johnnie this chance and thank God I chose rightly. I had to do it this way because I knew that you would refuse,' he paused, then added more gently, 'but don't think I enjoyed you not knowing and I am glad that Paul told you today.'

Kate turned away from him to lay her hand on the cool trunk of a tree as if its texture would bring her comfort.

She said, 'You're not going to stop him, are you?'

'No.'

'You've never been hard like this before.' She turned to look at him. 'I told you — Paul has changed you too.'

'Perhaps he has. I hope so. He has anyway, made me see how weak I've been all these years, made me see what I should have done long ago.'

'He's taken *you* away from me as well as Johnnie.'

Dell stood very still, looking at her.

'Not unless you want it that way.'

She didn't answer but her hand remained on the tree, moving restlessly up and down.

Dell moved nearer to her.

'Kate, I love you. You know that. But this is right and I *must* do it. Try and see it this way.'

Again, she didn't answer and after a moment, Dell turned and walked slowly back to the house. He had triumphed by remaining firm but, torn between his wife and son, he wondered sadly just how much it had cost him.

7

Dell had been awake most of the night, searching and worrying for some solution to the problem which every day was becoming more acute. It was a month since Paul told Kate of their programme for Johnnie and during that time, they had steadily grown apart.

Kate's continued policy of waiting on Johnnie made it difficult for the boy to maintain any independence without becoming involved in rudeness to his mother. Dell was still torn between his sympathy with Kate and his determination to free his son from her influence.

It was almost with relief that he heard the telephone ring about five in the morning. He glanced at Kate as he put down the receiver. She hadn't moved and he thought she really was asleep at last. Night after night, they had lain silently awake side by side but there was no communication between them and they might just as well have been miles apart.

Sliding out of bed, he dressed quietly and quickly. The call was an emergency and it was his night on duty.

He returned to the house about ten-thirty to bath and shave. Kate offered him breakfast but it was too late and he wasn't hungry.

In his consulting-room, Lise had a list of patients to be seen and the necessary case cards laid out ready. At the bottom of the list was Laura Denham's name with an added note from Lise. 'Rang about nine. Tummy pains. Would like you to call this morning. Don't think anything urgent.'

Arranging the order of his calls, Laura Denham came last but one and he arrived at Thelby Hall shortly after twelve. The door was opened by a woman he knew by sight.

'Mrs. Denham's in the drawing-room,' she announced and took him through the hall and opened the door.

His patient was lying back on a divan with pillows piled behind her. She held out a hand and smiled.

'Oh, Dell, this is good of you to come so soon and, at the moment I feel such a fraud — no pain at all. It must have been the thought of you coming.'

'Well, that often happens.'

'Yes, but you see, I was frightened. Silly, isn't it? But the pain really was rather much and of course, I immediately thought of everything dreadful which could happen to me. You know how it is.'

'Being frightened isn't silly.'

She looked, as she always did, immaculate and immensely attractive, her smooth fair hair falling slightly forward. Laura was a beautiful woman and knew it. She looked up at him now, blue eyes appealing. Dell and Kate had known her socially for about two years since she had bought the delectable Georgian house called Thelby Hall. Professionally, Dell had only attended her once about five months ago, and that had been for a sprained ankle.

'How long have you had this pain?'

She made a small grimace and began undoing buttons.

'On and off for about a week — across here.' She demonstrated with a hand across her diaphram.

Dell questioned her, then made a careful examination.

'Nothing much wrong except the rich food you say you eat. You will have to go on a strict diet.'

'Oh Dell — how utterly shaming. You make me sound like some awful glutton. I suppose I am, really, but you see, I'm lucky, I never put on an ounce of weight, so I never have to be careful what I eat.' She smiled wryly. 'Now I suppose you are going to be brutal and cut me off all the things I like best.'

She swung her legs off the divan in a lithe movement and stood up.

'I don't care what you say though, we're going to have a little drink to celebrate this dreadful diet. I insist on that.'

Dell watched her walk gracefully across the room to a table on which stood a bottle of champagne already on ice. Picking up the bottle, she held it out to him.

'Please do it, I'm no good at this.'

For a second, Dell hesitated, then shrugged.

'You know you shouldn't be doing this, and nor should I, but I imagine that nothing I say will make any difference.'

She laughed, crinkling her eyes at him.

'How right you are. This is a pleasure on which I insist. After this, I promise to do everything you say.'

He drank the first glass slowly, feeling it reviving him. He watched her refill the glasses, feeling more relaxed than he had for some time. He continued to sit there, drinking the champagne she poured. He was suddenly very tired.

Smiling at her, he said, 'I had a very early call this morning, this is doing me a lot of good — putting fresh life into me. I feel a different man.'

Laura regarded him with sympathetic eyes.

'Dell, my dear, you work much too hard. You must tell Kate to take more care of you. From what I can see, you need more cherishing.'

At any other time, he would have resented this obvious slur on Kate. Now, after a sleepless night and half a bottle of champagne on an empty stomach, he seemed to be seeing things in a different light. Laura's sympathy washed pleasantly over him and he felt gratitude seeping through him although he hastened to assure her that Kate worked hard too but it was only a half-hearted attempt to spring to her defence.

Laura agreed smilingly. 'Oh, I know Kate works hard, but so much of her time is taken up with looking after poor Johnnie.' Pausing, she laid a hand on his arm. 'Dell dear, don't be cross with me but I really do think that Kate worries too much about him. I wish

— well — I wish she thought more about you. You need taking care of as well, you know.'

She felt the muscles of his arm tighten and pressed it briefly before taking her hand away and saying wryly, 'Oh, I'm sure you feel like hitting me, but you know the old adage, lookers on see most of the game, and it's very true. I'm very fond of dear Kate but I do think that she should see that you deserve as much consideration as Johnnie.'

She looked at him pleadingly.

'You must forgive me. You see, I'm a lonely person myself and I can't help knowing that you too, are lonely. I — I suppose I shouldn't be saying this.'

She put out her hands towards him and involuntarily, he took them in his own, gazing down into those guileless blue eyes.

'Please forgive me,' she repeated in a low voice. 'I just wish I could do something to help.'

Dell, dropping her hands, said

brusquely, 'There's nothing to forgive. It's kind of you to be so concerned though you need not be.'

'Well, of course I'm concerned. We've known each other some time now, long enough to call ourselves friends and I always say that friends should help each other whenever possible.'

Turning away, Dell sat at a small table to write out a prescription, then handed it to her.

'That should help but remember what I said about a light diet. I really mean that.'

Laura smiled disarmingly.

'Oh, I'm sure you did. You're being utterly brutal, but of course, you're quite right and I'm just a greedy pig. I promise you I'll be very obedient. You're coming to see me tomorrow, aren't you?'

Dell hesitated, watching that eager face.

'Well, you know, it's not really necessary.'

'Oh, *Please*. You can't abandon me

94

like that. Please come. You've made me feel different already — no pain.'

As Dell started his car, he was conscious of feeling a trifle flushed and giddy. On three glasses of champagne? He was annoyed with himself for breaking his rule of never drinking on duty and he supposed he felt giddy because he hadn't eaten since the previous night.

He had one more call to make on his way home and he was abruptly and uncomfortably aware of old Mrs. Brompton's sharp eyes on him as he questioned her about her condition. He was perfectly sober, what was she staring at?

Driving slowly home, he thought about Laura. She was a lovely woman separated from her husband. She had too much time on her hands, rich, with enough money to buy Thelby Hall and furnish it expensively and with impeccable taste. He and Kate constantly met her locally and they had dined in each other's houses several times. Today, she had spoken of herself as a friend. Was she a friend?

He frowned. The phrase 'setting her cap' came into his mind. Not a conceited man, he was usually quite unconscious of the fact that women found him attractive. The fact being so obvious today, troubled him. Laura had said she was lonely. He believed her, yet it did not fully account for her manner to him. And himself?

He slowed to turn off the main road, drove slowly down the lane, finally stopping outside the surgery. Switching off the engine, he continued to sit in the driving seat.

Well, what about it? There was no harm in what he had done. And she *was* lonely. She said that his visit had done her good. With an irritable movement, he opened the car door, got out and went into the surgery, slumping down into the chair by his desk.

His head ached and he didn't have to search far for the reason. He tried to make his mind a blank but it didn't work. Always honest with himself, he was unwilling to accept anything less than that now. He sat back, seeing himself clearly in Laura's drawing-room, forcing himself to face the thoughts which had been in his mind then. She had not only been a patient. He had been acutely aware of her as a most attractive woman; he had watched appreciatively as she walked over to the drinks table.

He leaned forward, his hands over his face. He was being ridiculous. It was just the champagne. He had been stupid and wrong to drink it. He never drank while he was on duty. Why had he done so today? He had suddenly felt exhausted and dispirited. Was that the reason? Was that enough reason?

No. The real one; the only one, had been because he enjoyed drinking it with Laura. It was as simple as that and he had to accept it. He pushed his fingers through his hair as he stood up. Well, it mustn't happen again. Suddenly, as he picked up some notes Lise had left on the desk, he saw just how corny the whole scene had been. How could he have fallen for such a patent set-up. The attractive housecoat, the champagne already on ice, the guileless eyes gazing up into his; the sympathy. How could he have been so silly? Surely he was too old to be taken in by such obvious wiles. But, apparently not.

He stood for a moment, looking through Lise's notes without really seeing them. Finally, he smiled wryly. He had to admit that it had been a pleasant interlude; nothing more. He had met this sort of thing countless times before and dealt with them quite easily and he had no doubt that he could deal with this. He looked up to see Lise standing in the doorway telling him that lunch was ready. He smiled at her, suddenly realising that his head-ache was nearly gone and surprised to find that he was feeling hungry.

8

By the next morning, Dell had decided on making an excuse to send Paul to see Laura in his place, but when he went into his consulting-room to tell him, Paul had already gone.

As he closed the door of the empty room Dell wondered wryly if he had subconsciously left it too late to contact his partner. Whatever his reason, he now had to go himself. He made it his first visit. She could scarcely offer him champagne at ten o'clock in the morning. He was determined to keep the visit formal.

But when he drove away from Thelby Hall about ten-thirty, he was not absolutely certain that he had done so. In spite of his own formal manner, Laura had managed to introduce a certain intimacy into the conversation and as soon as he told her that it was not necessary for him to call again, had tried to persuade him that she needed him.

'You are on the phone,' Dell told her with a smile. 'If you have any further attacks, you can let me know. In the meantime, carry on with the treatment.'

Even that, she had managed to turn into a sort of triumph for herself by patting his hand as he said goodbye, nodding her head and saying in a low voice, 'Don't worry Dell dear, I understand.'

Angrily, he drove from the house, annoyed with Laura but more so with himself because he recognised a degree of regret in his own decision not to visit her again. But if she phoned? After all, she was a patient. Dell drew up at his next call and with determination, pushed the incident from his mind.

At home, Kate went about her jobs with a sense of misery. For the first time in years, she had time on her hands and she seemed to have no idea how to use it. Practically all the small time-consuming things she did for Johnnie, he now did himself and it was constantly borne in on Kate that she was less and less necessary to him. Although she constantly searched for signs of strain in the boy, she could find none and admitted even to herself that he really was better in every way. When she allowed it to, that gave her pleasure but in her mind was the new anxiety of her relationship with Dell. Never had they been so far apart, and for that, as for everything else, she blamed Paul, still not admitting that the original fault was her own.

Because of all the years of bondage to Johnnie, Kate had no close friends, no one at all to whom she could turn for the comfort and advice she so badly needed. She felt, and was, entirely alone. She found it a curiously frightening sensation which sent her scurrying out into the garden where at least there were early autumn jobs waiting to be done. The warmth of the sun on her back soothed her as she worked and the thoughts which she couldn't stop took on a slightly less negative quality and even had a sort of depressing construction.

It seemed that without any doubt, she must accept this entirely new concept of Johnnie. Dell had, for once, proved himself stronger and more determined than she so there was little hope of returning to her former life.

Viciously, Kate snipped at a dead rose, throwing it with unnecessary force into her gardening basket.

Since she was not prepared to condone Dell's behaviour, what was the alternative? Reluctantly, she saw that the only one was to remain as they were.

Kate stood, the scissors poised in her hand, her brows drawn together, her mouth tight. But she still loved Dell. The cold thought crept in that perhaps Dell no longer loved her. Could he have acted in this way if he had?

She wandered aimlessly down a path

between two borders. That idea was a new and chilling one. For years she had taken him for granted, followed her own wishes for Johnnie without hindrance from him but now she would have to reconstruct her own image of Dell and see him as himself, not merely as a husband who gave way to her in everything, and this made him into a stranger. A handsome, hard-working man whom she scarcely ever saw alone. Except at night when, in a routine which now seemed absolute, they lay silently side by side in the big bed. Yet, in spite of everything, she could not entirely accept the fact that he had stopped loving her. Dell wasn't like that; Dell was the type who loved for ever. But because of this new situation, he was learning to do without her.

Kate stood very still, half-listening to the shrill sweet notes of a robin in a branch above her. Suddenly she turned and walked quickly back to the house, clear at least, about one thing. If that was the way Dell wanted it, she must learn to do without him too.

It was only when she reached the house that she realised that tears were streaming down her face. She heard the study door open and Philip and Johnnie come out and she ran swiftly upstairs to her own room to stand by the window, letting the tears run unheeded down her face.

Confused and bewildered by the changes which were taking place, she could not yet find any formula by which she could take up her life again. Nobody needed her; nobody wanted her, yet she must struggle on because she loved her family and they were necessary to her; her only wish was to look after them.

In a moment of sudden enlightenment, it occurred to her that perhaps that had been her trouble all along, yet, wasn't that what a wife and mother was for? Dell had always appreciated that she had run his house efficiently, that she had always been there to welcome him and feed him when he came home tired. Had all that gone, as well as Johnnie's need of her? Would Dell notice if she were not there when he came in?

She moved restlessly away from the window. That, at least, was easy to prove. Abruptly and surprisingly, she decided to go up to London the next day. Preferably without explanation. There was plenty of food in the house and Lise would have to cook it.

Kate knew perfectly well that it would be an everyday experience for most women but for her, it was a momentous one. Something she had not done for years. If everything was changed, she was going to change with it. She glanced in the mirror to see what damage the tears had done. Not enough, she thought with bitterness, for her unobservant family to notice. Nobody would really see her. She looked critically at her own face, something she rarely bothered to do. Searching closely, there were a few lines around her eyes and mouth, but other than that, Kate didn't think she had changed much.

Suddenly she smiled at her image, wondering pleasurably what she would wear tomorrow and where she would go. When she went downstairs, she saw that there was a letter lying on the hall mat. It was addressed to her and she opened it.

'Dear Kate,

'I am having a small dinner party on Tuesday night next week and would be so pleased if you and Dell can come. It is quite ridiculous when we live within a mile or two of each other how seldom we seem to meet. I do hope you are able to make it, about eight o'clock.

Yours, Laura.'

She stood with the note in her hands as she heard Dell come into the hall.

'This is from Laura,' she said, holding the note out to him. 'She wants us to go to dinner next Tuesday.'

He glanced at her sharply. 'Do you want to go?'

'Why, yes, it would be nice. Don't you want to? Can't you manage it?'

He said, ignoring her first question, 'Yes, I think I can manage it. If you want to, we'll go.'

He started to go upstairs, then turned back to her with a smile.

'How about a new dress for the dinner? I'll make you a present of one. Would you like that?'

He looked down at her face from the first step and was surprised to see sudden tears in her eyes and she bent her head as she answered him.

'Oh, Dell — that would be lovely.'

'Then go up to town and make it a really good one. Choose one the colour of your hair.'

She stood watching him as he ran up the stairs, her feelings confused. Why had he suddenly made this suggestion? He wanted her to have a dress to match her hair. It was the sort of thing he used to do when they were first married. But now? Was he doing it because he still loved her and wanted to please her, or was it merely a placating gesture for what was happening between them? She simply didn't know but she thought with wry irony that her proposd defiant decision to go off to London had been swept from under her by Dell's suggestion about the dress. With mixed feelings, she made her way to the kitchen and commenced cooking the meal.

9

The day in London had been a great success and Kate brought home a tawny dress of which all the family approved. Lise insisted that she put it on for them to see, then walked round her, tweaking it into place.

'It's terrific, it really is. Takes years off you.'

Johnnie said cheekily. 'Mum. You look quite a dish in that. Doesn't she Dad?'

Dell laughed, 'Well, you shouldn't describe your mother that way, but, yes, she looks, as you say, quite a dish.'

Kate gazed at them all. It was wonderful, they were all together, entirely without tension and with real affection. She felt grateful to Laura for making this possible, for, without her invitation, it would not have happened.

Johnnie glanced at his watch.

'I'm meeting Paul at the station at nine-thirty.'

In spite of himself, he couldn't keep the importance out of his voice. The previous day he had passed his driving test and although with driving Paul so much, he had become quite experienced, this would be the first time he had taken the car out alone.

Kate turned to him.

'Oh no, Johnnie. Not tonight. Not in the dark.'

There was an instant's silence, then Johnnie laughed.

'Oh, Mum, don't be daft. I've been driving in the dark for ages. You know that.'

'Not by yourself.'

'I've passed my test. They wouldn't have passed me unless I'd been O.K.'

Kate said, 'There's no need for you to go. Paul can take a taxi.'

'A taxi? When his own car's here and I promised to meet him?'

After its short absence, tension was back in the room. The lighthearted mood gone as if it had never been. Dell said, 'I'll meet him if you like,' knowing that Johnnie wouldn't accept.

'No thanks Dad. I'll go.'

He went out of the room, closing the door quietly.

Kate stood, her eyes on the closed door, then, abruptly, she turned and walked out of the room in her new dress.

After a moment's hesitation, Dell followed her and Lise was left alone. She was worried and uneasy, aware of all that Paul was doing for Johnnie, but confused as to its effect on the relationship between her parents. Kate came back into the room, changed into her usual clothes.

'He shouldn't have gone.'

'He's all right. There's nothing to worry about.'

Before Kate could reply, the telephone rang and she rushed to answer it, standing silently listening, then she said, 'But he left here in plenty of time to meet the train,' then, as she realised what she was saying, her voice rose hysterically. 'I *told* him not to go. He's had an accident. It will be your fault if he's killed.'

Lise heard the click of the extension phone in the study and Dell came into the room.

'The car may have broken down. It may not be an accident.'

Kate said impatiently, 'Of *course* he's had an accident. No one would listen to me.'

Dell regarded her with a kind of hopelessness. In a controlled voice, he said, 'If there's been an accident, the police will inform us, but I'll take the car over the same route.'

He was on his way out as she said, 'Shall I come?'

'No. You stay here in case there's a message.'

Kate was right. There had been an accident. On the cross-roads just before the station, Paul's car was slewed across the road, the offside buckled. Dell drew up and got out of his car, his heart pounding, in that moment realising how much Johnnie meant to him. Suddenly he was aware that Paul was at his elbow saying, 'Johnnie's all right. The chap with the van jumped the lights. It wasn't Johnnie's fault. There are two witnesses, one of them a policeman. Johnnie's here,' he said, leading Dell across the road.

The boy stood leaning against the wall while he gave particulars to the officer who had witnessed the accident. He looked white and shaken. As Dell approached, he said, 'This is my father,' and, turning to Dell and Paul, added, 'How did you both get here?'

Paul said, 'I phoned from the station when you weren't there and I imagine your father came along as soon as I'd phoned.'

The officer smiled at them.

'He did a good job. Very nearly managed to miss him. It would have been much worse if he hadn't kept his head. Chap came straight through the red light.'

'What happened to *him*?' Dell asked.

'Head went through the windscreen. The ambulance has just left. The van's a write-off.'

'Paul, I'm sorry about your car.' Johnnie's voice was anxious and at once Paul put a hand on his shoulder.

'It wasn't your fault, anyway.'

Dell, seeing a phone call box, went to call Kate. She must have been waiting by the phone.

'Johnnie's all right. A van ran into him on the offside.'

'Dell, I *told* you he —'

'Kate,' Dell said patiently, 'this was not Johnnie's fault, there were witnesses. Don't worry. We'll be back soon and I daresay he could do with a hot drink when we arrive.'

He knew she would feel better with something to do for Johnnie and, as far as he was concerned, they could all do with a drink. He wondered if she would try and blame Paul, but when they arrived home she was so concerned with ministering to Johnnie that she scarcely noticed the two men.

* * *

Johnnie was shaken and bruised and for the next few days found Kate's ministrations almost acceptable. He could accept them because the need for them had arisen out of an accident which could have happened to any normal person. Privately, he was pleased with his own reactions. He had remained calm throughout and done the right things, but he admitted to himself that he had been lucky that a policeman had been there to witness what had actually happened.

Once he was over the shock, he ended up feeling a trifle important about the whole thing, feeling in a curious way that it was the first time he had competed with normal people on the same level. He knew and was pleased that he had come out of this test well and wondered if his father had remembered a half-promise to buy him a small secondhand car if he passed his driving test.

On Tuesday, at Laura's dinner party, there was only one other guest, Henry Maddon whom Dell and Kate knew. Dell, who hadn't wanted to come was relieved that Laura kept the conversation general, making some laughing comments on the rules which he, as her doctor, was supposed to have laid down for her.

'Of course,' she said, her smile directly for him, 'he was too polite to say so outright but it was quite obvious that he regarded me as the most undisciplined greedy pig. And,' she waved a hand in Kate's direction, 'having made that clear, he completely abandoned me — brutally left me to carry on with no further help. *Quite* heartless, don't you think?'

Again, it was directed towards Kate who said hastily, 'But you are so slim already, you certainly don't need to lose any weight.'

Laura shook her head.

'No, no. I don't need to lose any weight. I never do, but your hard-hearted

116

husband put me on to this horrible diet because he said I was ill purely because I was greedy.' She turned to Dell, touching his hand briefly. 'You did, didn't you Dell?'

Watching him, Kate wondered why he should look embarrassed as he picked up his wine glass. Smiling, he said after a moment, 'I certainly don't remember being quite so discourteous, I merely suggested that you should eat plainer food. Quite a different thing.'

Henry Maddon used that as an excuse to compliment Laura on a delicious dinner.

Laura assured him that she liked cooking.

'It's a pleasure to provide a meal for guests. I'm not like poor Kate who has to cook for a family every day as well as look after Johnnie.' She paused, eyebrows raised at Kate. 'How is dear Johnnie? I couldn't believe my eyes the other day when I saw him driving. I wondered, you know, if it was quite *safe* — I mean — '

'Johnnie has passed his test, so presumably, he is entirely safe.'

Dell's voice was sharp and cold and again Kate looked at him in surprise while Laura remained unperturbed.

'Clever boy to pass first time. My apologies for doubting him.'

She smiled disarmingly at Kate, adding jokingly, 'You'll find yourself out of a job if you're not careful now that Johnnie's becoming so independent.'

Kate's eyes flicked towards Dell.

'Johnnie is certainly much better. He's beginning to do much more for himself. It's wonderful, really.'

Dell knew what the admission must have cost her, recognised the near reluctance in her voice, realised too, that it was more in the nature of a peace-offering to himself than a general statement and he smiled at her across the table.

Later, when the two men joined Kate and Laura in the drawing-room, Laura said gaily, 'I've been complimenting Kate on her new dress. It's quite modern — quite with it — I think it suits her, don't you?'

Kate seemed unaware of the condescension in Laura's voice but Dell was conscious of a sudden surge of anger.

'Of course it suits her. She always chooses what is just right for her.'

His voice was again cold and he saw Henry Maddon glance quickly at Laura, and Kate's small, puzzled frown as she looked at him. But Laura, unabashed, was handing coffee to her guests and the next instant, Henry filled an awkward pause by changing the subject entirely.

'I saw Philip in his new Jensen Healy last Friday. He's a lucky young man to be able to afford a car like that.'

Glad of the change of subject, Dell said quickly, 'I imagine he must have private money, he certainly couldn't run it on his tutoring.'

The conversation became general and the rest of the evening passed pleasantly enough. When they were leaving, Laura put a quick hand on

Dell's arm as she turned to Kate.

'My dear, you must look after Dell. He works much too hard. I thought he looked terribly tired when he was here the other day. Now that Johnnie is more independent, perhaps you will find more time to cherish him a bit.'

Before Kate could answer, Dell said, 'You forget that I have a partner now. I'm not nearly so hard worked as I used to be,' and Kate added, 'No, he actually has time to sit down quietly to a meal now.'

She looked at Laura doubtfully, uncertain of her manner and wondering why it should be making Dell so on edge as he twitched his arm from under her hand. Laura turned innocent eyes on him.

'That's good. Perhaps next time you visit me, you won't have to rush away so soon.'

With a wintry smile Dell said, 'Well, if you stick to plain food and not too much of it, I shan't need to visit you at all.'

For a second, her eyes were cold, the next she was wishing them good night and expressing pleasure at their appreciation of the dinner.

In the car Kate said, 'You weren't very nice to her. What was the matter with you? I thought you liked her?'

He wanted to say, can't you see that she was trying to make you look small, but instead, he said, 'Oh, she's all right — too much money and too little to do — that's her trouble. It's a pity she can't do something more useful than think about her own health.'

He wondered what Kate would do if he told her that Laura was gunning for him in a big way. Would she believe him? Would she mind if she did? He glanced quickly at her profile in the light of a passing car. Tonight, perhaps because she had enjoyed herself, she looked serene, the anxious lines smoothed from her face and for that instant, he felt closer to her. He dropped a hand over hers as they lay in her lap.

'Did you enjoy it? Your dress was a success, wasn't it?'

'Yes — a lovely dinner and Henry's nice, isn't he?' And then, almost as if she was afraid of their intimacy, 'I do hope Johnnie's all right. I hope he went to bed early. He needs the rest after that terrible shock.'

Dell replaced his hand on the steering wheel and with a perverseness which he knew would finally shatter this mood, he said, 'I bought Johnnie a little car today,' and felt her stiffen beside him.

'Oh Dell — how *could* you do such a thing. You're only encouraging him. He might have another accident.'

'I bought it because I promised him and because it will do him good to have that independence.'

She didn't answer and without looking at her, Dell knew that her mouth would be tightly held and the anxiety lines back in her face. Mentally, he shrugged. He had brought this on himself by telling her about the car, but she had to know sometime and her reaction would always be the same.

When they reached home, Kate went straight upstairs and Dell heard her knock gently on Johnnie's door. After a moment, it opened and she went inside.

10

In the surgery, the phone rang and Lise left the message on her father's desk.

'Mrs. Denham would like to see you as soon as possible. Suffering from stomach pains.'

When he saw it, Dell's first reaction was anger, his second pleasant anticipation, instantly squashed by the thought that perhaps Laura really was ill.

'I haven't been making a pig of myself, so don't be cross with me.'

She smiled at him from the bed but it didn't take Dell long to discover that she was not suffering from any pain. Deliberately, he kept his manner entirely professional.

Suddenly she pulled his face down to hers as he leaned over her, pressing her mouth hard against his, forcing him off balance. For a few seconds, his body lay against hers, the next instant he was pushing himself upright, very conscious of her scent and the fact that his heart was beating furiously. With anger? With excitement? He didn't know.

When he was free, he stood back, looking down at her. She shook her head ruefully.

'Oh, my dear, why do you fight so hard? What harm could it do to have a little happiness together? Nobody need know. I doubt if Kate would care. She doesn't appreciate you and I — '

Dell put out a hand to stop her.

'Stop. Enough harm has been done already.'

Laura stared at him, assessing his mood. He had responded to her kiss and now she judged his words as a conventional reaction which she felt certain she could overcome.

'You must forgive me Dell, but I just knew you felt the same way as I do and — ' she left the sentence hanging, waving a helpless hand. 'I want you so much — Kate doesn't deserve you. I could make you so happy. Where would be the harm?'

She looked very lovely, her eyes pleading and he stood fighting the temptation to take her in his arms. She hastened to take advantage of his hesitation.

'Dell, you *do* want me too, I know you do.'

Suddenly anger came to his rescue and he said in a shaking voice, 'Do you want to ruin me? Think what you are saying. What do you think would happen?'

'Nothing. Nobody would know.'

'And Kate?'

She made a derisive gesture.

'Kate wouldn't know either.'

'No. We can't.'

It was a tacit admission that he wanted to but he only knew that he must get out of this room as quickly as possible before weakness and desire took over. He walked to the dressing-table, snapping his bag angrily.

'Dell, you can't leave me like this.'

He turned to look at her.

'I must. You know that. What sort of man would I be?'

She held out a hand but he ignored it.

'My sort of man. You're my sort of man. You may as well face it.'

He stopped abruptly, her words penetrating his brain. Was she right? Her type, or Kate's?

'No,' he said, panic in his voice. 'Leave me alone. Just leave me alone.'

He went quickly out of the room and down the stairs and Laura felt a sense of triumph. She could wait.

In his car, Dell mopped his forehead, his body shaking. He wouldn't see her again. Paul would have to go. He would think it odd; he might guess. Round and round went the senseless, unrewarding thoughts which solved nothing. He felt trapped. Nobody could help him. It should be simple. He only had to choose between right and wrong. He still loved Kate. It should be easy; instead, it was the most difficult problem he had ever had to face.

* * *

A whole month passed without Dell seeing Laura. She had phoned once and when he had seen the message, he had asked Paul to go. His comments afterwards had been very much to the point. 'Nothing wrong that I could find. A hypochondriac with too much time on her hands.'

Dell had had a heavy day, November had started cold and wet with flu already prevalent. He entered the surgery just as the phone rang. He picked it up without thought of Laura in his mind.

'Dell? Oh, my dear, I'm so glad it's you. I feel so ill. I think it must be flu. Will you come?'

The impact of her voice was like a physical blow. He had made it plain enough to Laura that he had no intention of doing what she wanted and he had during these last weeks, begun to feel almost secure. And now this.

He held the receiver away from his

ear as if he hoped the gesture might break the connection and he wouldn't have to say anything.

'Dell — are you there?'

Her voice came tensely and he experienced a sense of panic. Paul was off duty for the week-end. Dare he refuse to go? He began to question her. Unless she was lying, she really needed a doctor. He would have to go. He looked at his watch. It was nearly eight o'clock and Kate would be expecting him to be ready for a meal. He went through to find her in the kitchen.

'I have to go out again.'

'Oh, no. I heard you come in and everything's ready.'

'I'm sorry Kate. I'll try not to be long.'

He drove fast and entered the house by the back door which Laura had left open.

He glanced at her flushed face, listened to her quick breathing. No, she hadn't made him come for nothing this time, she was really ill and frightened as well, and Dell felt a swift sympathy for her.

'Oh, Dell, can't you stay with me?'

He shook his head.

'You know I can't do that, but won't your woman from the lodge come in?'

Laura turned her head restlessly on the pillow.

'I don't know and she's not on the phone.'

'Then I'll go and ask her.'

'Why can't you stay? Oh, please.'

He said again, 'You know I can't,' and left the bedroom to contact Mrs. Bond who worked for Laura and lived at the lodge. After some argument, she agreed to sleep in the house and Dell returned to the house to tell Laura of the arrangement.

She said pathetically, 'You *will* come again Dell. *Please* don't send anyone else. Promise you won't.'

'I'll come in the morning,' he answered shortly, feeling as he did so that he was setting a trap for himself. 'These tablets should help and try to sleep. Mrs. Bond will be here in about half an hour.' Saying a quick good night, he went downstairs and out to his car, surprised to find when he got there that his hands were shaking. A feeling of hopelessness swept over him as he started the engine. He had thought he was over the worst and now he was committed to seeing her again. As soon as he entered the house, he poured himself a stiff whisky, and then another before going to find Kate. Normally, he never discussed patients with her, but tonight, he felt a compulsion to mention Laura.

'I'm sorry. Is she very bad?'

'Pretty high temperature and some chest congestion.'

'Will that Mrs. Thing look after her properly?'

'Yes, I arranged for her to stay in the house tonight.'

Kate was pouring hot soup for him. Because he was tired he was feeling the effect of the two whiskies that he had drunk too fast. Kate glanced quickly at him.

'Go and sit down and I'll bring you your dinner.'

He carried the bowl of soup into the dining-room and it suddenly came into his mind to wonder if Laura would be willing to keep a dinner hot for him if he were late. He put the bowl on the table and stared at it. Whatever had made him think of such a thing?

'Drink that while it's hot. Don't stand looking at it.'

Kate stood with a steaming plate in her hand. Dell looked at her and smiled with the sensation that he was returning from a long distance.

'I'm sorry Kate. Thanks for keeping it hot.'

He had the guilty feeling that she must know what he was going through, that the struggle must show in his face. Yet, nothing had happened; nothing was going to happen, but for the next three days he called at Laura's house, keeping his visits on a strictly professional level, but well aware that she had not given up the fight.

The fourth day, it was six o'clock in the evening before he was able to get round to see her. She was sitting by the fire wrapped in a very attractive housecoat. A tray of drinks was arranged on a small table beside her. Although she still looked ill, Dell decided that it would be all right if he left several days before calling again. After only a few minutes pleading lack of time, he said he must go. Laura left her chair and stood close to him.

'Dell?'

For answer, he started to turn away, but before he could do so, she flung her arms round his neck, raising her face to his.

At that moment, Mrs. Bond opened the bedroom door and came into the room. In a violent gesture, Dell tore at Laura's arms while the woman stared and smirked.

'I'm sorry, I'm sure, to disturb you. I didn't know the doctor was still here.' Mrs. Bond's voice was silkily artificial and turning his back, Dell picked up his bag. It took all his courage to walk past her to the door. Driving straight home, he poured himself a stiff drink, then swiftly, another. Cursing himself and Laura indiscriminately, he made his way to the surgery.

Earlier in the day, Johnnie had sought out Paul.

'How busy are you?'

Looking up from his notes, Paul saw that Johnnie held some papers in his hand.

'A Play?'

Immediately Johnnie looked embarrassed.

'Only a rough draft.'

Paul glanced at his watch.

'I needn't go out for twenty minutes or so, but I can't pretend to be any sort of literary critic.'

'I know — but I'd like you to see it first.'

Paul was aware of the compliment being paid him and held out his hand. Johnnie sat quietly while he read. Once or twice, Paul turned back to a page but he read silently until he had finished, then put down the MS. on his desk. Johnnie waited tensely.

'The theme's good. I think perhaps that some of the dialogue is a bit too stilted — people talk a little more carelessly than some of your speeches.' Paul paused, looked at Johnnie and saw that he was disappointed.

'Don't misunderstand me, I'm not knocking it, I think it's good, but you can make it better if you work on it. What does Philip think of it?'

'I've not shown it to him yet. I wanted you to see it first.'

Paul smiled at him.

'Thanks, I don't know that I deserve your flattery. What about length? I mean, is this to be theatre, broadcasting, or television?'

'Television,' Johnnie said promptly. 'One of their short ones.'

'Then as soon as you've worked it up a bit, we'd better have a reading. You've only three characters, two men and one girl so, if we can get Lise to co-operate, we can manage.'

Johnnie's face lit up.

'That'd be great. Would you really? I mean, I know you've not much time.'

'I think it would be fun, though, mind you, I don't fancy myself as one of the world's great actors. It might help though, to have people speaking the lines.'

'Yes, I'm sure it would. Thanks, Paul, I'll get to work on it.'

Paul gathered up his notes, watching Johnnie as he moved. He still limped and always would, but he walked more easily, his back was straighter and he had lost the peevish look which had so spoiled his expression.

'By the way, have you any idea where Philip's home is?'

'Oh, somewhere near Ipswich I think. Why?'

'I only wondered because my people used to know some Cranstons.'

'But your family live in Devon, don't they?'

'Yes, they do now.'

Johnnie followed Paul out of the room, too full of plans for his Play to wonder why he had been interested enough to want to know where Philip had lived before coming here.

11

The letter came by the first post, the address printed by hand, rather unevenly and in very pale ink. Kate, wondering who had written it, put it down on the kitchen table until she had time to read it. She forgot about it until she was making coffee for Dell and Paul before they went out after surgery. She picked it up as she returned to the kitchen, slitting it open with her thumb. There was no beginning and no end; only a hand printed section in the middle of a sheet of plain paper in the same pale ink as on the envelope.

'Doctors shouldn't have girl-friends. Did you know your dear husband had one? Champagne and kisses in the bedroom too. What are you going to do about it?'

The first reading made no impression at all. The wording, the letter itself, was so improbable, so entirely unrealistic that Kate felt that it could have no connection with herself. She picked up the envelope. Perhaps it was wrongly addressed. No. It was for her. She read it again and this time, shock hit her. Even so, the note made no sort of sense because this could not be referring to Dell.

An anonymous letter. She had received an anonymous letter. It was unbelievable. It was the sort of monstrous thing which might conceivably happen to other people but never to oneself. But it had. She glanced sideways at it, without touching the contaminating paper.

'Girl-friend,' 'Drinks and kisses in the bedroom,' 'What are you going to do about it?'

Kate sat down suddenly, her hands over her face, shutting out the hateful words. Well, what *was* she going to do about it? That, at least, had to be decided. Only a few months ago, there would have been no question in her mind. Unhesitatingly, she would have taken it straight to Dell. But not now. If she took the letter to Dell now, she had no idea what his reaction would be. Supposing he thought that she believed the accusation, that could only make matters worse between them. Much worse. So, Dell must not know. That at least, was a definite step. What was the next one?

Trying to bring her mind to bear coldly and clearly, Kate realised that there were other alternatives. She could burn the letter at once and try and make herself believe that she had never received it. On the other hand, people who received anonymous letters took them straight to the police. For a moment, she imagined herself doing that, but only for a moment. It was unthinkable. No doctor could afford that sort of thing to happen.

She supposed that most people would have friends who could advise them. She hadn't, she thought sadly, any like that. In the early days, she and Dell had been so close that they didn't seem to need many friends and later, after Johnnie's illness, there had been no time for her to make any. So what was she going to do now? How was she going to deal with this loathsome thing so that it did no further harm?

In spite of herself, she imagined herself showing it to Dell, waiting for his anger, his violent denial of its foul accusations. She imagined his eyes, looking through and through her, trying to gauge what *her* reaction had been. Would he ask her if she believed it? And did she?

Kate turned away to the window so that she couldn't see the letter. Outside, the wind sent leaves scurrying in waves across the lawn. She watched them with a sense of despair. They signified the end of something, the end of a season, something to be regretted. Was this an ending for her too?

Sharply, she pulled herself together.

Surely she wasn't giving credence to the wretched thing. Yet, the thought had almost unconsciously crept in that there must have been something to make the writer put pen to paper. She thought too, of how much Dell had changed during the last months. But that had been Paul's doing. Because of Johnnie, hadn't it?

She ran her fingers distractedly through her hair. Why was she suddenly doubting him? Dell, who had always been a loving, faithful husband. How could he change enough to do this to her?

A wave of guilt suddenly ran through her. A loving husband — but had she always been a loving wife? But Dell must know that she was really devoted to him. With abrupt clarity, she remembered the times when he had wanted to make love to her and she had made the excuse that she was too tired. Her hands came up to her face. She was suddenly afraid. She had been so sure that he had understood. He knew how hard she worked, how much of her time was spent on Johnnie. But not lately, she had done so little for Johnnie lately. So? She thought bitterly that lately, they had been too far apart to make love. She pressed her fingers to her eyes, trying to shut out the image of Dell in the arms of another woman.

It was unthinkable, yet, paradoxically, she *was* thinking it, partly believing the evil of the letter without giving Dell the chance to deny it, yet, far apart as they were now, she felt that it was impossible to show him the letter when by doing so, she would be admitting that there was already a doubt in her mind.

Thousands of people for hundreds of years must have been receiving anonymous letters and known how to deal with them. Surely she should be able to cope with this one. Other people's problems always seemed to be a clear black or white, while her own seemed to be made up of so many complications that she couldn't see anything clearly.

She heard the surgery door open and close, Paul's step in the passage and she snatched up the letter and crammed it into her overall pocket. In another moment Paul would come through with the empty coffee cups. It was a morning ritual and meant that he and Kate had reached some sort of truce.

'That was as good as it usually is. Thanks.' He put down the cups on the draining-board.

'Paul — is anything wrong with Dell?'

It was wholly impulsive, something unexpectedly said out of fear. Kate couldn't even explain what she meant by it.

He looked at her curiously and took his time about answering so that she felt tension build between them.

'What makes you ask?'

His voice was so cautious that immediately Kate wondered if he knew something. She tried to make her voice casual.

'Nothing special, I didn't think he

looked too well.'

She realised as she said it that it was true. True, and she hadn't noticed. 'You see, he never complains.'

'No. He certainly never complains.'

Paul's voice held an unmistakable note of criticism.

'*Is* he ill?'

He moved over to the window, trying to break the tension between them.

'No — not ill, though not terribly fit either, I think.'

Kate said, 'He's been drinking more. Not a lot — he never does — but more.'

'Yes.'

There was a long silence before Kate asked quietly, 'Why? Is he tired or — ' she hesitated, 'unhappy?' She wondered as she said it why she should suppose that Paul knew.

'He's probably tired,' he answered slowly, then added coldly, 'as to being unhappy, you are the only person who can know that.'

Without allowing her time to answer,

he strode to the door saying abruptly, 'I must go,' and disappeared down the hall. Kate stood where he had left her, still wondering why she had asked him those questions. Had she learned anything from his answers. Her mind flew to the letter. 'Drinks in the bedroom.' Dell *was* drinking more, which was unlike him.

She heard him coming through from the surgery. He put his head round the kitchen door.

'I shan't be back for lunch.'

Kate said to the fast retreating head, 'Where are you going then?'

There seemed a long pause before he came in to stand poised just inside the door. He said rather stiffly, 'I have a consultation over at Matheton and I shall have to take the chap out to lunch afterwards.'

Kate said, 'Have a good lunch then,' and wondered why she didn't believe him. She thought sadly as she heard him walk away that perhaps it was a pity she knew him so well; well enough to be certain that he had been lying.

Dell, as he drove away, thought that she hadn't believed him. He was a bad liar and during their marriage they had always told each other the truth. For one wild instant, he was tempted to go back and tell her everything. A temptation instantly squashed because it concerned a patient.

He was going to meet Laura in Matheton, a town about ten miles distant. For a moment, he wondered if she would come, but since she didn't know his reason for asking her to lunch with him, he thought it fairly certain that she would turn up.

When finally, she did arrive, she looked more lovely than he had ever seen her. He stood up as he saw the waiter directing her to his table.

'Dell, this is delightful. I thought you had deserted me.'

Dell said a little stiffly, 'I am glad to see you well again.'

He was annoyed to find his heart pounding at the sight of her but was still determined to carry out his intentions.

The waiter handed them both a menu and Laura chose carefully, shooting him a reproachful glance.

'You see how obedient I am. I have only ordered the things of which you approve.'

'Then I hope you enjoy them. What wine do you like?'

'How odd that you don't know,' she smiled. 'I mean, odd that this is the first time we have been out together.'

Dell didn't answer but studied the wine list, trying to make up his mind whether to let her have her lunch in peace or to tell her now the reason he had asked her to meet him. He decided to wait and tried to listen to her prattling. Apparently it was her policy completely to ignore the scene in her bedroom. That of course, was the easy way out; the way he could not take.

'That was a lovely lunch Dell dear,' she said as the waiter served coffee.

Dell said, 'I am glad you enjoyed it. I

148

am sorry to have had to bring you all this way in order to discuss what has to be discussed.'

She looked at him with dancing eyes, sure now that she had won him over at last.

'My dear, that doesn't matter. One must certainly be discreet; you can rely on me for that.'

Dell looked down at his coffee cup, turning the spoon round and round between his fingers.

'I don't think you *do* understand.'

His voice was quiet and Laura glanced sharply at him. This was not quite the tone she was expecting.

She said, 'I'll do whatever you want. You know that.'

Dell sighed. It was going to be more difficult than he'd hoped.

'You don't seem to realise that that woman could ruin me.'

'Darling — oh no — there's no question of that. I mean to say — we weren't *doing* anything. Besides, I can — '

She had been going to say, 'I can pay her not to say anything,' but glancing at his face, she let the sentence tail off.

'Whatever we were doing must stop. Can't you understand that?' His voice was cold and decisive and she looked at him in genuine surprise.

'Dell — my dear — don't be silly. What *are* you saying?'

'I am saying this must stop.'

Laura gazed intently at the table, deliberately not meeting his eyes.

'What must stop?' she asked demurely.

Dell moved impatiently.

'You know perfectly well, but if you want, I will spell it out for you. You are a very attractive woman with far too much time on your hands, so you decided that it might be amusing to have an affair with me.' Dell paused, met her eyes as she looked up. 'Only, you chose the wrong man because I happen to be in love with my own wife.'

There was a long silence while they stared at each other and Dell was intrigued by the various expressions passing over the lovely face opposite him. Undisguised disappointment, anger, and finally, a sort of sly acceptance which made him instantly suspicious and uncomfortable.

With a shrug, she said, 'You know, of course, that you are being very insulting, but you are so — naïve — that I imagine you can't understand what you are throwing away, and of course,' she treated him to a forgiving glance, 'in a way I admire your loyalty. It's just such a pity that it is so undeserved.'

Her hand came out to touch his across the table.

'Oh Dell, can't you see how Kate's *used* you all these years? Can't you see that only Johnnie matters to her and you simply don't count?'

Gently, Dell removed her hand.

'That is not true.'

Laura gave a mocking laugh.

'Oh, my dear, you must be blind.'

She gathered together her bag and gloves, stood up and looked down at him.

'We could have so much together. You don't suppose that I don't know that it's not all on my side. You wanted it too — you can't deny it.'

Dell pushed back his chair sharply and stood up.

'I am not denying anything. I am only telling you quite clearly that there is nothing — nor will there ever be anything — between us.'

His voice was quiet and very convincing and, seeing the genuine hurt in her eyes, he felt a moment's sympathy.

'You accused me of insulting you. I think you must know that that was not my intention.' He spread his hands in a helpless gesture. 'You must realise how hard this is for me, but my only concern is not to hurt Kate, and I have no intention of doing that.' He put a hand briefly on her arm. 'Please try to understand. I am sorry if this has hurt you.'

She put her hand for a moment over his.

'Poor Dell,' she said pityingly. 'You're making a terrible mistake.' She turned swiftly and without saying goodbye walked gracefully the length of the restaurant. Dell saw her give the head waiter a dazzling smile as he opened the door for her.

12

Dell sat down again at the table, ordered himself another brandy. It was done. The difficult and dreaded task he had set himself was finished. He took a gulp of the brandy. And what had he left? Two brandies later, he still hadn't decided. Looking round the restaurant, he saw that his was the only occupied table. Slowly, he stood up, beckoning the waiter and paying his bill. The figures on the paper weren't very clear to him but he managed to get out of the restaurant fairly creditably. As the cold air hit him, he realised that he was in no condition to drive and sat quietly in the car, going over in his mind the conversation with Laura. Most vivid in his mind was the memory of her beauty as she sat opposite him.

He moved impatiently. She certainly been right in thinking that he wanted her. Was it anything more than physical attraction? No. Nothing more. Well, he'd had the strength to remain faithful to Kate. In thought? In body, at any rate, and he supposed, hoped, that that was at least something.

Did Kate deserve his loyalty? Yes, of course. He leaned forward impatiently and started the engine.

Driving through the town, he saw that there was a complete blockage of traffic, with police and an ambulance ahead. For a wild moment, he wondered if Laura could have had an accident, but with the arrival of further police, he realised that the commotion was connected with the local bank and was not a road accident. He managed to back the car and drive down a side street, in no mood to sit in the car until the police had dealt with the matter. If the Bank had been raided, it would be the third in the area within six months. Curiously, the thought of so much crime didn't seem to concern him at the moment. He had closer things to worry him, things to which he apparently had no answer. He stopped the car at a cottage on the new estate outside the town.

'It's David. He's got a high fever — he's ever so ill.'

The small bedroom was overheated and stuffy and Dell was aware of his head spinning. He made a desperate effort to control it as he leaned over the child on the bed. He examined him with his usual care then went over to his bag. Once again the dizziness overcame him and he fumbled in his bag for the drug he needed, forcing himself to fill the hypodermic syringe accurately. His hand shook as he gave the injection but he managed to reassure the mother and to get himself back to the car, driving slowly home and letting himself into the surgery.

He sat down heavily at his desk feeling extremely ill, a sense of deep depression battering at him. After a few minutes, he went into the dining-room and mixed himself a drink. When Paul came in, he was sitting at his desk in the surgery, his hands covering his face. In front of him, his bag lay open.

Paul stood for a moment in the doorway staring in surprise at his partner. He came slowly into the room and Dell took his hands away from his face to stare at Paul. After a moment, he gestured towards the bag on the desk.

'It wasn't right,' he said thickly.

Suddenly Paul realised that he was not ill but that he had been drinking. He looked at his partner with cold deliberation. There was more here than that. There was a sort of despair in Dell's face for which no amount of drinking could account. Paul felt a sudden surge of sympathy as Dell looked up at him, gesturing towards some notes on the desk.

'I mus' go back.'

Paul shook his head.

'No. You can't do that. Just sit still.'

Dell picked up the notes with a shaking hand.

'Look,' he said carefully, thrusting them towards Paul. 'See — I gave him that.' He pointed to the paper and Paul read quickly, then, without pause, picked up his own bag and was already on his way to the door.

'How long ago? When did you give him the injection?'

' 'Bout an hour.'

His voice hard, Paul said from the door, 'You know what effect it will have, don't you?'

It was odd how deadly his quiet voice sounded. Dell shook his head.

'Can't think how,' he began and Paul chopped the sentence midway.

'You were drunk — that's how. If that child dies, you will have killed him.' The next second, he had gone, letting the surgery door bang behind him.

Ten minutes later, he rang the bell of the cottage, having had no time to plan how he would explain this sudden visit. This was not a patient with whom he had come in contact.

As the door opened, he could hear a

child crying and the expression on the mother's face told its own tale.

'What do you want? I can't see to anything now. I — '

'Don't worry Mrs. Channing — I'm Doctor Quest — Doctor Manley's partner. He asked me to call in. After he left you, he thought of something further to ease the boy. He's out on an emergency himself but he didn't want to wait until he could get here. Shall we go up?'

Smoothly done and effective for he saw her anxiety lessen as she turned to the stairs.

'It's good of Doctor Manley. I know he was worried about David. He seems worse and he's in a lot of pain, crying too.'

Paul looked at the child threshing about on the bed. All the symptoms he had feared were there, but he thought with vast relief as he examined him, that with any luck, he was in time. He gave him an injection and stood by the side of the bed waiting for its quietening effect.

'Oh, Doctor, will he be all right?'

Paul smiled at her, still holding the small wrist. Already the pulse was beginning to steady and he was conscious of deep relief.

'He'll be all right Mrs. Channing. He will sleep now and he'll be feeling a lot better when he wakes up.'

Mrs. Channing looked at him gratefully.

It was, he thought, so easy to reassure them. You opened a bag, produced pills or a syringe filled with a magic potion and one or the other would be capable of turning tragedy into the miracle of continued life.

'He wasn't as bad as this when Doctor Manley saw him.'

Paul gave her a sharp glance. Had there been a note of suspicion in her voice?

He said smoothly, 'No, this stage generally makes its appearance pretty swiftly.'

'I wish doctor had warned me.'

With relief and self-confidence returning, Mrs. Channing was feeling the need for a little oblique criticism. A mood which caused Paul a momentary alarm. He said a trifle coldly, 'He certainly wouldn't do that, Mrs. Channing. There would have been no possible point in alarming you.'

'No, but I mean — if you hadn't come —'

Paul snapped his bag shut decisively and smiled at her.

'Ah, but I did. I told you, Doctor Manley asked me to come at once. He knew that he had this drug at the surgery and that it would shorten the period of stress — and so I came along and,' he turned to the bed, 'you can see, he is better already.'

The hot staring eyes were closed now, the breathing more even, the dark flush receding. Paul drew a deep breath of relief as once more he felt the child's pulse.

'You've nothing more to worry about. Just take good care of him.'

For the first time, she smiled at him.

'Oh, I'll do that all right. It's such a relief. Thank you doctor, for bringing the medicine so quickly.'

Going down the stairs, Paul said, 'One of us will look in tonight,' and he knew well enough which of them it would be.

In the car, he sat for a moment almost weak with relief, then suddenly, he was shaken by a bitter anger against Dell. That he, of all men, could do this. A man who had always been so dedicated that even in these days of impersonal medicine, he had kept his ideals and stuck to them. Something pretty drastic must have happened to cause this breakdown.

Paul knew well enough the strain under which Dell had lived for a long time, knew also, that he had learned to live with it by the simple expedient of letting Kate have her own way. But not lately. He himself had changed all that. But although Kate had made things difficult, and at first, been antagonistic, he thought that the worst was over and that she was beginning to come round and admit to herself at least, that what was being done was right.

Paul stopped the car in the drive and went into the surgery. Dell still sat at his desk, but now he was asleep, breathing heavily, his head on his chest. Paul suddenly felt grateful that it was Lise's day off and Kate not here. What would they think if they saw Dell like this? He remembered Kate saying that morning that Dell was drinking more. She knew that much, so, today, he thought grimly, was not an isolated case.

The phone rang and Dell stirred but did not wake. Paul picked up the receiver.

'I'm sorry, Doctor Manley's not available but this is Doctor Quest, I'll come along right away.'

He heard Kate put down the extension from the house and hoped that she didn't know that Dell's car was standing in the drive. But Kate did know. She had seen Dell when she finally came to a decision about the letter. It had been the decision of desperation and largely because she could not think what else to do. Perhaps she was influenced too by the fact that she knew Dell had lied to her that morning. After he had gone, the hateful doubt had grown bigger, more definite. In the end, she had found herself searching in her mind for a name to link with his and as soon as she realised what she was doing, she knew she must try and clear the doubt away once and for all by showing the letter to Dell. Whatever their present relation-ship, however angry it made him, it now seemed imperative that he should have the chance to refute all that the letter had implied.

It seemed hours before she heard his car and listened for his steps. The sound of his stumbling frightened her, filled her with an unknown dread as he went into the surgery.

Standing stiffly in the hall, Kate tried to make up her mind to go in to him and when finally, she did, she was scarcely surprised at what she saw. Dell was sprawled in his chair, elbows on the desk, his head in his hands, his whole attitude expressive of utter hopelessness.

Kate's feelings in that moment were confused and complex. Her first instinct was to rush to him and hold him close, to comfort him in any way she could. This was closely followed by the certainly that she must not do anything of the kind. Dell thought himself alone; she must respect that privacy. She stood silently, waiting for him to move, hoping that he would become aware of her presence. Unwilling, hateful thoughts flooded her mind, compelling her to assess coldly what she was witnessing.

That Dell had been drinking was obvious and, to her mind, equally obvious that only extreme emotional strain would bring him to this level. The sort of emotional strain brought about by a situation such as that mentioned in the letter. Kate, feeling her legs trembling, turned and quietly left the room. In all the confused sadness of her mind, one thing stood out clearly. She couldn't show him the letter now because now she knew that it contained at least some truth. Dell must remain unaware that she had any knowledge of what was happening. In an obscure way, she had the conviction that Dell must be free to fight this in his own way. Fight? What made her so certain that he *was* fighting? Perhaps only her knowledge of him during all the years she had lived with him, perhaps because of his look of utter dejection as he sat at his desk.

She walked slowly away to fight her own battle, to struggle to come to some conclusion as to what her own part in this was to be. What sort of woman was she fighting? What sort of woman would Dell find attractive enough to risk his whole future and the happiness of his family? She didn't know. Dell had always been an exemplary husband. She had no experience to help her. She only knew with sudden certainty that she was prepared to fight with all her strength to keep Dell's love, and to this end, she realised that she must work out some sort of campaign. Such as what, she wondered helplessly.

She walked over to the mirror in the bedroom, examing critically the reflection she saw there. She leaned forward. A few wrinkles around the eyes, but her jawline was still taut, the muscles of her neck didn't sag and her hair remained as bright as it had ever been, and she hadn't put on weight.

On the other hand, she hadn't taken enough care of her appearance. Her dressing-table was practically destitute of the jars and bottles other women seemed to accumulate and of which she had been inclined to be a trifle scornful.

She took a brush and tried swirling her hair a different way. It didn't stay. Her hair was naturally curly and wilful. Going into Lise's room, she experimented with the jars she found there, looking again searchingly at her reflection. It was definitely an improvement. Returning to her own room, she changed her dress, pausing as she pulled it over her head. Why was she doing this? Why was she bothering? If she really had lost Dell's love, what difference would it make?

She tried to push the feelings of hopelessness away as she fastened the dress. She was jumping to conclusions. This morning at breakfast, everything had seemed normal. Only after the arrival of the letter was everything changed. Perhaps she was exaggerating its importance. But Dell, sitting there with his hands hopelessly over his face must mean something. The lies he had told her, they had to mean something too.

With a feeling of utter depression, Kate walked downstairs to the next task of the day.

13

Philip brought the car to a flourishing standstill in the small car park behind the restaurant in Matheton.

'It's certainly quite a car,' Lise told him. 'You really go to town over cars, don't you?'

'Yes, I've always been keen, and I've always wanted to own one of these.' He patted the front of the Jensen Healey affectionately.

Lise said almost as a question, 'You're lucky to be able to afford it,' and for answer, he merely smiled as he walked with her towards the restaurant. They were a little early and there were still several empty tables. Philip ordered drinks and then looked at his watch.

Lise said, 'We've plenty of time, haven't we?' and he nodded. They had planned to go to a cinema after a leisurely lunch.

'Have you read Johnnie's play yet? You know he wants Paul and me to do a reading with him? Do you think it will be any good?'

Philip laughed. 'What a sisterly remark. Why shouldn't it be? Johnnie's clever you know, and he's changed out of all recognition since Paul got to work on him, also, I think he *has* the ability to write.'

Lise sat for a minute not speaking and when she did, it was on a different subject.

'Philip, what are you going to do when you've finished tutoring Johnnie? Are you going on teaching?'

He looked at her sharply.

'No. Most definitely not that.'

'Then, what *are* you going to do?'

He smiled at her across the table.

'I want to travel.'

'Yes — well — holidays but, I mean, what sort of career do you want?'

It occurred to her as she watched him that she had never asked him anything like this before.

Still smiling, he said, 'I don't know. I've never really thought about it.'

Lise stared at him incredulously.

'Not *thought*? But you must *know* what you want to do. I mean — '

He answered evasively, 'When I finish with Johnnie, I shall want a bit of time before deciding my next move.'

When she didn't answer, he looked up suddenly.

'Are you afraid,' he asked facetiously, 'that I shan't have enough money when I marry you?'

'Don't be silly. Of course I wasn't thinking of it like that but — '

'Only you'd like to be sure that I'm not penniless after buying the Jensen?'

Again he was laughing at her and she felt sharp annoyance. Philip leaned across the table, putting a hand over hers.

'Don't worry darling. There's plenty more where that came from, I promise you.'

For no particular reason, Lise felt uneasy. He had never volunteered anything about his financial position, and until he had bought the Jensen, she had never really thought about it, more or less taking it for granted that his salary was all he had. Obviously, she had been wrong and he must have a considerable private income.

'Does this sudden interest in finance mean that you have finally decided to marry me?'

Lise shook her head, immediately feeling guilty. Why couldn't she decide? She knew that she was being unfair but seemed unable to come to a decision.

'Let me wait a little longer Philip. Please.'

He picked up his drink and finished it before asking crossly, 'Five years — ten — twenty?'

She made a helpless gesture, then, watching him across the table saw his expression change. He flicked his eyes towards her, then away.

'What is it?'

For a second, Philip hesitated, then shrugged.

'Your father is lunching here.'

'How odd. He never said. Are you sure?'

She began to turn her head and at once, Philip said sharply, 'Don't turn round.'

She said in surprise, 'Why ever not?'

'Because he is with Mrs. Denham.'

Lise sat very still, her mind racing. Laura was a patient. She was also a friend. There was no real reason why he shouldn't take her out to lunch. Only, why hadn't he said? And why wasn't her mother with them? It didn't seem the sort of thing he would do. She met Philip's eyes across the table.

'Lise, what are you thinking?'

'Nothing,' she answered far too quickly.

'You know that woman's been gunning for him for ages.'

She hadn't known and she suddenly felt her inside cringe.

The waiter was setting their order on the table, Philip was consulting with the wine waiter. She needed that moment to pull herself together. Abruptly, she realised what she *was* thinking and tried to shut her mind against it. Not her father.

When they were alone again, she said, 'I expect there's some reason why he's lunching with her. I mean, Dad wouldn't — '

She didn't complete the sentence and looked appealingly at Philip who said, 'She's a beautiful woman. And a very determined one.'

'Yes, but — '

'Better men than your father have been bowled over by women like that.'

'No.'

But into Lise's mind came the knowledge that there had been a definite change in the relationship between her parents. She had thought it was because of Paul and Johnnie. What if it had been this and her mother had known about it?

Philip said soothingly, 'I expect you're right. It certainly doesn't sound like your father.'

Lise turned her head quickly. Laura was leaning across the table to touch Dell's hand and Lise didn't have time to see Dell remove it before she turned away. She only saw that they appeared to be completely absorbed in each other and once more she felt that cringing fear inside. If this was an innocent meeting, why couldn't he have taken her to the restaurant in their own town?

'Lise darling, eat your lunch.'

She was conscious of the sympathy in his voice, which meant that he was thinking the same way as she. Deliberately, he changed the subject, talking about the film they were going to see which had had a good write-up in the local paper, and all the time, Lise longed to turn round and watch that other table, yet hoping that her father would not turn this way and see them. Suddenly she became conscious that Philip had already looked at his watch three times. For some obscure reason, it irritated her.

'Why do you keep looking at your watch? We're not late.'

'No. We've plenty of time,' he said, not answering her question, but only a few minutes later, she saw him glance at it again and wondered why he was so on edge.

As they were being served coffee, Philip said, 'She's leaving. By herself.'

'Good. Has he seen us?'

'No. I'm sure he hasn't and we can go out of the sidedoor if you like.'

When they came out of the cinema, Philip drove down the main street. The traffic was flowing again but there was still a police guard outside the Bank and a few people standing about, telling each other about the raid.

'Look Philip — what's all the excitement? There's a police guard outside the Bank. Do you think there can have been a raid?'

Without slowing down, Philip said, 'Looks rather like it. I wonder what happened?'

He drove fast and when they reached

the house, he leaned across to open the door for her.

'Aren't you coming in?'

'No. Not now. I've some things I must get done tonight.'

Lise said in a small voice, 'I wish you could. I'm rather dreading meeting him.'

Philip looked at her with a puzzled frown.

'Him? Oh, your father,' he said, as if he had entirely forgotten the episode at lunch. For a second, he hesitated.

'I'm sorry darling, but this is rather important. I must go. There's nothing to dread. He won't know that you saw them.' He leaned over to kiss her on the cheek and with a sigh, Lise got out of the car.

'Well, thanks for the lunch and show, anyway.'

She watched him drive away and turned slowly towards the house. Dell's car was in the drive and she hesitated by the surgery door, finally going in and opening her father's door quietly. She stood just inside, gazing in surprise at the slumped figure at the desk. At first, she thought he was ill and went forward into the room but as soon as she reached him, she could smell the whisky and was conscious of a quick revulsion as she looked down at this man who was her father. That he was drunk, she could see; that he had drunk to this extent because he was unhappy, she had a sudden conviction and in spite of herself, her heart went out to him. She wondered if she should wake him. He was supposed to be on duty. The next instant, she realised that even if she woke him, he would be in no condition to drive a car and deal with a patient. She could only hope that there would be no urgent calls. She went quietly out of the room, closing the door behind her.

In her room, she sat on her bed, her whole mind absorbed with the problem of her father. After the visit to the consulting room, she had no further doubts what was happening to him. He was having an affair with a patient. It was unbelievable, but what other explanation could there be? Remembering that figure slumped at the desk she thought with some bitterness that certainly it was not bringing him any happiness.

14

It was late when Paul returned to the surgery. Normally, he would have gone straight home but he had to satisfy himself that Dell was all right. He pushed open the door of the consulting-room. At first, he thought the room was empty.

Lise turned from the window.

'I've made him go to bed.'

It was a statement which told Paul nothing of her knowledge of the situation and he hedged.

'Was he ill?'

Lise treated him to a scornful glance and he was struck by the drawn whiteness of her face.

'Ill?' She flung out both hands. 'You know, don't you? You know what was wrong with him? It's why you've come back.'

He pulled out a chair for her,

gestured to it, sat down himself.

'Yes. I know.'

Lise sat down wearily.

'Oh, Paul — what are we going to do?'

He took time to answer, then he said slowly, 'Find the reason, I suppose. So that we can help him.'

She looked at him in astonishment, forgetting that he lacked her own knowledge, and, now that she remembered, hesitated between loyalty to her father and her own need for help in a problem much too big for her. Paul studied her expression in the silence.

'*You* know the reason?'

He asked it quietly, almost as if he were giving her the chance not to tell him unless she wished. Lise nodded.

'But not until today.'

She sat with her hands tightly clasped in her lap, her head lowered while she came to a decision. At last she said, not looking at him, 'Philip and I had lunch at Matheton today.' There was a pause, then the rest came in a rush.

'Dad was there with Laura Denham.'

Paul met that with a long silence, trying to assess just what it meant. It could mean nothing; Lise obviously didn't think so. In the time he had known Dell, he had formed the opinion that not only was he a good doctor but that he was a good husband and that he loved Kate and would do nothing to hurt her. On the other hand, he was also aware that the situation he himself had brought about regarding Johnnie had caused strong feeling between Kate and Dell. This, he thought would heal when Kate realised and accepted the improvement in her son.

He asked tentatively, 'Is that so odd?'

'Of *course* it's odd. Dad doesn't *do* things like that and besides — ' she stopped abruptly, suddenly not wanting to commit herself.

'Besides?'

Lise shrugged helplessly. Now that she had started, she might as well continue.

'Well, they seemed completely absorbed

in each other — I saw her put her hand over his on the table.'

Paul said quickly, 'Not the other way round?' and she puckered her brows.

'Oh — you mean, she made the first move. Does that make it any better?'

'It might.'

Paul was suddenly remembering that Dell had once asked him, without any particular reason, to visit Laura Denham instead of himself, and he had formed the opinion on that occasion that she was a man chaser.

'Doctors are often placed in difficult positions by patients,' he said a trifle ambiguously and Lise latched on to this small ray of hope.

'You mean — she's been chasing him?'

'Yes.'

She was silent, looking down again at her hands, then she shook her head.

'She couldn't *make* him take her to lunch.'

'Did they see you and Philip?'

'No, and she left before he did.'

They both sat silently for a moment, Paul trying to assess, Lise struggling to find some excuse for her father's strange behaviour.

'I found him sitting here drunk. I didn't let him see that I knew. I let him think that I thought he was ill.'

'Yes, that was wise.'

'But, don't you see? All this is so unike him. He's never drunk much — he's never been interested in any other woman. I know he hasn't.'

'No. I believe you. As regards drinking. People often drink because they're unhappy and, as for the other — we don't know yet and we must give him the benefit of the doubt.'

'But Paul — what can we do?'

He accepted that 'we' but privately thought that it would almost certainly be he who would have to do something.

Standing up, he said, 'The first thing to do is to switch any calls for him through to me to-night.'

She said miserably, 'I'm sorry Paul. Please don't think too badly of him.

He's never done anything like this before. He's always been so marvellous.'

'I'm not thinking badly of him. We don't know what's happened yet. The most important thing is not to upset Kate. Did she see him?'

Lise shook her head.

'I don't think so. He was alone when I came in.'

'Well, so that's good. Leave the next move to me. I'll see what I can find out.'

She looked at him gratefully. He could understandably have been angry and impatient. Instead, he was being calm and helpful. Almost for the first time, she found herself liking this man who, up until now, she had regarded merely as a disrupting influence in all their lives.

'You won't tell Dad that I know, will you?' This seemed important to her and at once, Paul agreed.

In the morning, Paul waited for the first move to come from Dell. At the end of surgery, he came into Paul's room and closed the door standing with his back against it. Paul went on writing.

'It isn't much good apologising, is it?'

'What happened?'

Dell came forward into the room as Paul looked up. The older man pulled up a chair and sat down heavily. He looked haggard and miserable and Paul took pity on him.

'She's been chasing you, hasn't she?'

He heard Dell's long sigh of what he took to be relief.

'How did you know she was the reason?'

'You remember asking me to see her instead of you?'

'Yes.'

'It was fairly obvious that she was a nympho and I gathered that since you asked me to see her, she must be after you.'

Dell said dully, 'That sounds as if I cast you to the wolves.'

'No. I could cope. It was you she was after.'

186

'But I blame myself too.' Dell pressed his hand to his aching head then continued. 'I've never wanted anyone but Kate. You must believe that but — well — this business of Johnnie — '

'For which I am responsible.'

'And for which I am grateful, you know that, but for the moment, it hasn't made things easy between Kate and myself.' He paused, as if uncertain how to continue. 'It sounds as if I'm trying to make excuses. It's difficult to explain without — '

'She's a very attractive woman and that never makes this sort of thing easy.'

Dell looked at him curiously.

'It seems *you* are making excuses for me. Why?' For the first time, Paul smiled.

'Because I happen to believe you're not guilty.'

Dell's face showed complete surprise. Surprise and relief.

'Why are you so sure? No one would be — and I wouldn't blame them.'

'I know you pretty well now. I know

the standards you set yourself — and I've worked with you. It didn't fit, that's all.'

Dell pushed himself up from the chair, walked restlessly round the room and sat down again.

'Oh, Paul, if you knew what a relief that is. It's true. That is — I've never made love to her but — by God — I've been damn near it. I haven't come out of this well — I know that. It hasn't been easy; I don't feel proud of myself.' He made an almost violent gesture with both hands. 'But it's finished. I met her for lunch yesterday at Matheton and had it out with her. I think I've made it entirely clear that there will never be anything between us.' He paused. 'She wasn't pleased.'

Paul said drily, 'No, I don't expect she was pleased. Theoretically, she is still your patient. If she sends for you. I can go instead. She can scarcely make a fuss under the circumstances.'

'It would be good of you. I certainly don't want to go if it can be avoided.'

Dell sat silently for a moment, saying finally, 'None of that excuses last night.'

Paul said, 'The boy might have died.'

Dell shook his head.

'No. By the time you came it had got through to me what I'd done. I would have got there somehow.'

Paul thought, and if you had, Mrs. Channing would have realised you were tight and that would have been the end of you. He said doubtfully, 'I suppose you might have made it.'

Dell stood up.

'I am deeply indebted to you Paul — actually on many counts, but specially now and, believe me, I'm grateful. One thing I want you to know. This is finished. I've learned my lesson. I've been too near the brink to risk any more.' He paused and met Paul's eyes. 'Whatever comes now, I can handle it.' He leaned for a moment on the back of the chair.

'I am more thankful than I can say that Kate knows nothing of this. I don't know what would have happened if she had. It wouldn't have been easy to make her believe me — and who could blame her?'

Paul didn't answer, and after a moment, Dell turned to the door.

'Thanks again Paul, and I hope that one day, I can do something for you.'

Watching him go, Paul was conscious of a deep relief. He was not stupid enough to think that all trouble was over, but he believed Dell when he said that as far as he was concerned it was finished. He wondered briefly if Laura was prepared to accept his verdict meekly or if she would try to make further trouble. He thought that was an aspect which hadn't so far occurred to Dell who was for the moment, content to accept the triumph of his own decision as the final gesture. Paul could only hope that he was right.

He picked up his notes from the desk. He must tell Lise as soon as possible.

15

Kate was pleased with the idea of the cocktail party. Carefully, she made a list of people. At first, she was dubious about including married couples, but she reminded herself cynically that unfortunately, there was no rule that a married man should not be attracted to a married woman. So, those men with pretty wives were included. That left about four unattached women.

It was to be an informal affair and she telephoned instead of sending out invitations and she was pleased to find that all her intended guests were free to come.

Kate had thought up the idea the day after the anonymous letter. After finding Dell in the surgery that night, she had forced herself to accept the fact that the letter told the truth. Armed with this hateful knowledge, Kate became a fighter. If you fought, you had to have weapons with which to fight. The cocktail party was to be her weapon. She was convinced that when she saw Dell in the same room with those women, she would recognise the enemy by his manner. With craft she had arranged the party for his day off duty and she didn't tell him about it until shortly before.

When Lise had come to tell her that Dell had gone to bed because he didn't feel well, Kate had taken it for granted that Lise had really believed just that. Neither Dell nor Lise knew that she herself had visited the surgery and seen him.

She went about in a sort of numb misery which enabled her to go through the day automatically carrying out her usual tasks, and other than her plans for the party, she tried to live for each hour alone. When Johnnie came into the room asking her if she had seen Philip, his question didn't register and he had to repeat it.

'No, I haven't seen him. Why did you want to know?'

'Because he isn't here and it's nearly ten o'clock.'

'Perhaps he's ill,' she said vaguely.

'I doubt it. He's never ill.'

At lunch, Kate laid a place for him but was told that he still hadn't turned up. She tried to bring her mind to bear on this since it seemed to be troubling the others but couldn't help feeling that in relation to her own problem it was completely unimportant. That Lise was worried failed to make any impact on her. It wasn't until the afternoon that Philip's absence became a solid fact with which, whether she wanted to or not, she was forced into involvement.

The bell rang and when she went to open the door, two men stood on the step.

'I'm sorry to trouble you, but I believe Mr. Philip Cranston works here.'

Kate regarded them without curiosity, her mind still on her own troubles.

'Yes, he tutors my son.'

'Then, is he here?'

'No, I don't think so. My son told me he hadn't come this morning and he certainly wasn't here at lunchtime.'

The two men glanced at each other.

'Could you tell me when you last saw him?'

'Why, yes, I saw him yesterday. He took my daughter out to lunch in Matherton,' Kate said, wondering what this was all about.

Again the glances between the two men and it dawned on Kate that perhaps Philip had had an accident.

'Is there something wrong? Has there been an accident?'

Although she still could not bring herself to a vital anxiety, she suddenly thought of Lise and what she would feel about this.

The older man said, 'As far as we know, there has been no accident.'

'Then — ?'

'Perhaps we might speak to your son. He might know more about Mr.

Cranston's whereabouts.'

Kate doubted it but asked them in and called Johnnie.

'No,' he said to their questioning, he only knew that Philip had not turned up this morning. 'Why are you asking? Who are you?' Which was something it hadn't occurred to Kate to ask.

'We are police officers and we want to know Mr. Cranston's whereabouts about two o'clock yesterday afternoon.'

Johnnie smiled.

'That sounds very sinister but I can certainly tell you that because he took my sister to lunch in Matherton and then to the cinema.'

Kate's reaction to what Johnnie said was entirely different to that of the men. She had only just remembered that there was only one restaurant in Matherton and if Dell really had taken another doctor to lunch there, surely Lise would have seen them. Perhaps she could ask her casually.

She heard Johnnie say, 'I'm sorry I can't help you more and I only hope he hasn't had an accident. Have you tried his flat?'

'Yes. There was no answer. Could we perhaps, speak to Miss Manley?'

'Johnnie, tell Lise, will you?'

It was a new departure that Kate should ask Johnnie to run an errand instead of going herself but at this moment, she didn't think of that for she was busy planning how she could ask Lise about seeing Dell in the restaurant without arousing her suspicions. She noticed how pale Lise was when she came into the room and attributed it to her anxiety for Philip.

Looking at the two men, Lise asked at once. 'What's wrong, has Philip had an accident?'

'No, Miss Manley — not as far as we know. He just seems to have disappeared.'

Lise looked bewildered.

'Disappeared? But how could he? And why should he, anyway? Of course he hasn't disappeared — I had lunch with him yesterday.'

'Yesterday, yes. Can you tell me the

times you were with him?'

Lise glanced from one to the other feeling a sudden, uneasy dread.

'He called for me about twelve-thirty and we drove into Matheton in his car. We lunched and then went to the cinema.'

In her mind, she was trying to relate the questions to her father and Laura but could see no connection. And if there were none, then this must mean that Philip was in some sort of trouble. Trouble from which he had run out? No. Of course not. She was being absurd and melodramatic.

The older man consulted some notes.

'What time did you leave the cinema?'

'About five thirty, I think.'

'And what did you do then?'

'We drove back here.'

Without any known reason, Lise had a sudden vision of police outside the bank in the High Street.

'Did Mr. Cranston stay?'

'Stay?'

'Yes, did he come in with you when you reached home?'

Lise shook her head.

'No, he said he had work to do. He was tutor to my brother, you know,' she added, as if that explained it.

'Yes, and — ' the detective hesitated, then smiled, 'and were you and Mr. Cranston engaged?'

Lise looked at him in sudden annoyance.

'Engaged? NO, but I fail to see what that has to do with — ' she paused, 'with anything, and why are you asking all these questions if there has been no accident?'

'There was a bank raid yesterday in Matherton and we have reason to believe that Mr. Cranston was connected with it.'

Johnnie burst out laughing, Kate looked incredulous and Lise said sharply, 'What nonsense.'

'I hope you are right, Miss Manley. In the meantime, we have to make these enquiries.'

'But what time was the raid?'

'Between two and three o'clock yesterday afternoon.'

Lise's voice was both scornful and relieved.

'Then you're wasting your time. You know that Mr. Cranston was with me during that time.' She gave him a withering glance. 'Unless, of course, you are suggesting that Mr. Cranston and I carried out the raid ourselves?'

'I wasn't even suggesting that Mr. Cranston took part himself at all,' the detective said mildly.

'Then why on earth are you connecting him with it at all?' asked Johnnie indignantly.

'There were three men on the job. Two got away, but the third one was caught.'

The man seemed to think that the inference was clear and looked from one to the other.

Finally, Johnnie said, 'So?'

'This man mentioned Mr. Cranston. So we are anxious to interview him.'

Kate stood up pointedy.

'I am sure Mr. Cranston will be able to set your mind at rest as soon as he returns home,' she said, waiting for them to go, and immediately, they both got to their feet.

'*If* he returns home.'

Once again that feeling of uneasy dread struck at Lise, but she tried to make her voice light as she said, 'You make it sound as if he were trying to escape from something.'

The detective threw her a shrewd glance.

'Yes, it does sound rather that way, doesn't it? Well, thank you for your patience and I hope we shan't have to bother you again.'

Neither man shook hands with any of them, merely offering to see themselves out and after they had left, there was a long silence in the room until Johnnie, drawing a long breath, asked, 'Well, what do you make of all that?'

Kate said crossly, 'How absurd. How can they waste their time like that?'

But Johnnie was watching Lise, surprised by her tightlipped silence.

'Of course he was with me. We had lunch, I told you and — '

'He *was* with you?' he asked suddenly and she moved sharply.

She had been on the point of saying that her father had been there too but pulled herself up in time. This was Kate's cue.

'Dell said that he might lunch there with a consultant he had to meet. Perhaps they were there at the same time as you and Philip.'

It was definitely a question and one which Lise had to answer.

'I didn't see them,' she said with exact truth and wondered what had caused her mother's question, then realised that he must have told her that was what he was going to do and instantly her fear for Philip became entangled in pity for her mother and a feeling of hopelessness swept through her. Everything seemed to be collapsing round her. She was conscious of

Johnnie watching her, of her mother's anxious face, but knew that her anxiety was not for Philip.

Johnnie asked, 'Do you know what this is about?'

She shook her head wearily.

'I haven't a clue,' she said and turned to leave the room before he could ask any more questions.

In her own room, she paced restlessly wondering why she wasn't entirely sure that the police were wrong. Why had she this sneaking doubt about Philip? And where was he now? She thought back over the last weeks. To the two or three occasions he had excused himself on her day off, saying that he had urgent business so he couldn't take her out. Suppose; just suppose that those men were right. Philip had a brilliant brain; just the sort of brain which could plan every detail of a raid like that. It would have to be organized over a long period. Suddenly, she thought of the new car, of Philip saying, 'There's plenty more where that came from.'

Sharply, she tried to stop her thoughts. This was the man she was contemplating marrying. Philip would be able to explain, until then, she must believe him innocent.

16

During the next twenty-four hours, there was still no sign of Philip and by the end of that time, Lise was certain that he would not return. Although she kept telling herself that he could have had an accident, or something else befall him, she held a deep conviction that none of these things had in fact, happened. The detectives were right. Philip had simply disappeared. And the only possible reason for that was that he was guilty.

She remembered suddenly, his preoccupation with his watch, her own feeling that he was on edge. That would have been about the time of the raid. She recollected him slowing down outside the bank, then suddenly picking up speed and her mind registered the fact that he had not even glanced towards the bank when she had mentioned the police on duty.

Lise sat at her desk at the end of surgery, her hands holding her aching head. She had scarcely slept.

'Lise, I want to talk to you.'

She hadn't heard Paul enter the room and now she raised her head wearily.

'Oh, Paul. *Now?*'

'Yes. Now.'

He sat on the edge of the desk, leaning forward to take both her hands in his.

'I wanted you to know as soon as possible that as far as your father is concerned, it is entirely finished.'

She looked up at him, her eyes uncertain.

'But he took her out to lunch.'

'I know — that was the reason for it. He told her quite clearly then that he wasn't interested.' He paused. 'Lise, he never has been interested.'

That this was stretching the truth, he was aware, but he knew that Lise would interpret it in the way he intended.

'You mean, he never — ' Lise stumbled, hating to put this into words connected with her father. Paul rescued her.

'I mean that there was never anything between them. Though I am quite sure that that was not Laura's fault.'

He saw tears of relief come into her eyes and after a moment, she said quietly, 'Thank God. Now Mummie need never know.'

Paul let her hands go and stood up.

'There's something else.'

Looking up at him, she saw the concern in his face.

'It's about Philip.'

Her expression changed to eagerness and hope.

'You know where he is? You've seen him?'

He shook his head.

'No. Nothing like that I'm afraid.' He hesitated, watching the hope fade quickly.

'Philip's family used to live in Ipswich when *my* family lived there.'

She was watching him now, a wary expression in her eyes.

'You mean, you *knew* him?'

'No, *I* didn't know him, but I knew *about* him.'

She received that in silence and Paul continued.

'When I came here, I had no idea that it was the same Cranston. I didn't connect it up until one day when he was talking about cars and it suddenly reminded me.'

He paused and Lise said, 'Reminded you of what?'

'Stolen cars. There was a spate of them, all round Ipswich.'

Suddenly angry, Lise asked, 'Are you suggesting that Philip stole them?'

'Not quite. There was never enough proof to pin it on him. He always worked through other people. He only did the planning.'

There was a long silence.

'After that, Philip disappeared. The pattern's the same, you see,' he finished quietly.

'But it *can't* be the same man. I'm sure — ' She threw out a hand without finishing the sentence, almost as if already, she couldn't believe what she was saying. Suddenly, she looked at him accusingly.

'If you knew all this, why didn't you say something about it? Why didn't you tell me?'

Paul came to stand in front of her.

'And if I had? Would you have believed me? You don't even believe me now. I could have offered no proof. Besides — ' He stopped, looking down at her with sudden sympathy. 'Besides, how could I when I thought you were going to marry him?'

Lise sat silently, trying to cope with what he had said.

'But — if you *knew* — '

'I didn't. Cranston's not such an uncommon name and — I told you — I'd never met him. It wasn't until I asked Johnnie where he lived that I was certain that it was the same man.'

He sat again on the corner of the

desk, his eyes on Lise.

'And then,' he said slowly, 'I couldn't make up my mind what I should do. It was a difficult decision. There were so many complications.'

After a moment, she agreed quietly.

'Yes, I can see it was difficult. I wish, though, you had told me.'

'What difference would it have made?'

Lise shrugged wearily. 'I should have been better prepared for this, shouldn't I? It wouldn't have been such a shock if I'd had previous doubts.'

As she spoke, she realised with finality, that she had accepted the fact of Philip's guilt. She didn't know yet, what that would do to her; whether it would entirely kill her love for him. She didn't even know just how deep that love had been. Why had she always hesitated to commit herself? Had she even then, had doubts about him? It was easy to imagine that that had been the reason, but the hesitation had been definite and she realised now with a sense of surprise that even in this moment of shock, she was experiencing almost a sense of freedom.

'I know this must be a terrible shock, and I'm sorry. I wish I could do something to help, but I'm afraid there's not much hope of that.'

She gave him the beginnings of a smile.

'You've helped about Dad — enormously. Just think what a relief that is. I was so terribly afraid that Mummie would find out, and I know what that would do to her.'

The telephone shrilled beside her and that meant that they were both back on duty. Lise leaned across to pick up the receiver.

'Thank you Paul, anyway.'

Somehow Lise managed to carry on during the next days. Further visits from the police made it clear that Philip was implicated. The man who had been caught made a definite statement naming Philip Cranston as the organiser; not only of that particular raid, but of the others which had been recently carried out all round the district. Unexpectedly, it was Johnnie who was the most understandingly sympathetic.

'This must be pretty rotten for you but, have you thought — if he could go off like this and leave you without a word — he can't be worth much. I mean, you couldn't *marry* a man like that, could you?'

'I know. But, how could I tell? He always seemed so — gentle. *You* liked him, didn't you?'

Johnnie said slowly, 'Yes, I *liked* him, but I wasn't *fond* of him. He was a marvellous teacher and I admired him tremendously but — ' he hesitated, frowning, 'but you know, I was never all that keen on you marrying him, though I couldn't have told you why. I was just glad that you didn't seem to be in a hurry to decide.'

Lise looked at him with new eyes, suddenly realising how much Johnnie had grown up during the last months. That this was directly Paul's influence, she didn't doubt.

He said now with an odd conviction, 'You weren't *really* in love with him, were you?'

'I honestly don't know. I certainly thought so.' She moved restlessly round the room, 'but it gives me the oddest feeling to think that I was so nearly engaged to someone who could treat me like this. Somehow, it doesn't seem real.'

'No, I feel that too. Someone you've seen every day and thought you'd known, and then — well — they're not what you believed at all.'

Lise glanced at him sharply.

'This must have been beastly for you too,' she said and he nodded.

'Yes. Rather rotten, actually though,' he hesitated, almost as if he was surprising himself, 'Well, I mean, it's nothing like so bad as if it were Paul for instance.'

'You'd mind that more?' she asked, surprised.

'Well, of course. Paul's marvellous.

Just think what he's done for *me*, besides — ' again, he hesitated, 'besides, he's a different sort of man altogether.'

Lise watched her brother's face.

'How so different?'

The thin hands moved eloquently while Johnnie tried to find the right words to express what he meant.

'He's — well — so *strong*. He gives you confidence all the time.'

Thinking about that, Lise admitted that perhaps it was true. What she had taken for arrogance, could be strength. She remembered Paul's arrival and its effect on Johnnie, the change in the boy from that moment; change which had turned him from a rather fretful semi invalid into a determined and cheerful young man who had every intention of overcoming his disabilities in every way he could.

Against that was the fact that Paul's influence had brought unhappiness to her mother and worsened the relation-ship between her parents, and this was something she deeply resented, looking upon it as Paul's unwarranted interference. Now, thinking about it in the light of what Johnnie was saying, she was inclined to change her opinion. Surely it couldn't be wrong to do what Paul had done for Johnnie and, that being so, you couldn't blame him for its effect on anyone else.

And Laura? Was she prepared to blame Paul for that too? But, if Paul hadn't come, would it have happened? She moved irritably and Johnnie said, 'You don't like him, do you? You never have.'

He made it a regrettable statement of fact and involuntarily, Lise smiled.

'You make me sound pretty difficult to please.' She paused, wanting to make clear her feeling about Paul, as much to herself as to Johnnie.

'Don't think I'm not grateful to him for all he's done for you. I agree, he's been wonderful, but — ' she realised suddenly that she didn't want to discuss their parents with Johnnie who, perhaps, was unaware that there was anything amiss between them. 'Well — it's just that he's a bit high handed and that takes a bit of time to get used to.'

'But you still disike *him*,' Johnnie persisted. 'I don't see how you can.'

Recollecting how Paul had handled her father's problem, and her own relief, she said slowly, 'No, I don't really disike him any more. I expect it's just that he's not my type.'

Johnnie stood up with his usual awkwardness and for a moment, gazed at her speculatively.

'Well, don't kid yourself that you're his type either,' he said with brotherly candour and limped slowly out of the room.

Lise, watching him, realized with equal candour that she had always taken Johnnie for granted; someone who had to be waited on and looked after but never to be taken seriously. Until now, when her eyes seemed to be opening to a great many things, she had never really considered him as a person in his own right, one who was capable of evolving opinions to which other people listened and which were of some serious account. Was that of Paul's making too? Reluctantly, she admitted that probably it was. Altogether, as a family, they seemed to owe Paul Quest rather a lot.

17

It was not until the morning of the cocktail party that Kate told Dell that she had 'asked a few friends' to drinks. Dell was mildly annoyed to have his free day messed up but beyond that, was not particularly interested. Afterwards, he couldn't understand why he had not thought that Laura would be asked.

Lise was surprised that her mother had suddenly elected to have a party, but as it was not her own day off, she had no time to speculate on the reason and barely time to change her dress and only came down just in time to join her parents as the first guests arrived.

Lise regarded Kate in frank astonishment. She was wearing a new turquoise and white dress which set off her lovely colouring and her hair had obviously been styled specially for the party. Dell,

Lise noticed with pleased amusement, was giving Kate covert and admiring glances of which she seemed totally unaware.

Soon the room was more than half full and people were still arriving. Lise turned towards the door to see Laura standing just inside. She stood quite still, staring across the room and Lise didn't need to turn round to know that she was looking at Dell.

Lise's glance went straight to her mother who was talking to a group of people while her eyes travelled restlessly round the room. They came to rest on Dell who stood transfixed. Slowly Kate turned towards the door. After only a momentary hesitation, she excused herself and went to meet Laura, taking her directly over to Dell.

'Give Laura a drink Dell, will you? If you'll excuse me, I can see someone else arriving.'

Lise was standing motionless in the middle of the room, feeling entirely unable to move. She felt a hand under her elbow, urging her towards a table on which stood several appetising dishes.

'Unfortunate.'

Paul spoke quietly and she looked at him despairingly.

'What are we going to do?'

'Just behave normally. Remember, your mother has no reason to suspect anything. Just leave Dell to deal with it.'

But Paul watched Kate's head turn from Dell towards Laura and suddenly wondered what she had thought in that moment. For the first time, a doubt came into his mind. Could she possibly have any clue to what had been happening? He turned to watch Dell and Laura standing together, saw Laura put a hand on Dell's arm. He couldn't hear what he said to her but it didn't please Laura because he saw her frown. The next minute, Paul was crossing the room to join them, carrying a plate of sandwiches with him.

'Good evening, Mrs. Denham, can I offer you one of these? I can recommend them, they're delicious.'

The brief, barbed glance she bestowed on him was certainly not one of welcome.

'No thank you.'

Turning her back, she pointedly addressed Dell, saying something about the success of the party.

'So clever of Kate to organise it so well.'

Before Dell could reply, Paul moved round to face her, saying pleasantly, 'As far as Dell and I are concerned, it was a surprise party. Neither of us knew about it until this morning.'

For the first time, Laura really looked at him and he saw the sudden flash of anger. Mrs. Denham, he thought with relish, could put two and two together and come up with the right answer and he held her eyes with his own until she finally looked away, then he turned to Dell with a smile.

'I think the drinks are getting a bit short over there, do you want to do anything about it?'

Without looking at him, Dell said, 'Yes, of course, I'll go and see to it.'

Laura watched him walk away, and Paul watched Laura. She was very angry, but for the moment, she could do nothing more than move away from him without another word. Glancing round the room, Paul saw that Lise was watching him. She was smiling at his successful dislodgement and he raised his hand in acknowledgement before joining another group.

Lise picked up a plate which needed refilling, carrying it out to the kitchen. Seeing her mother's overall hanging on the back of a chair, she put it on while she cut more sandwiches. When she had finished, she stood for a moment, her hands in the pockets while she considered the position which had arisen. Her father hadn't known about the party, and in any case, one glance at his face would have convinced her that the last thing he wanted was to be confronted with Laura. On the other hand, it was only natural that Kate should ask Laura to the party.

Lise was holding a piece of paper as

she took her hands out of the overall pockets. Supposing it to be one of Kate's shopping lists which she was always mislaying, she put it on the kitchen table. The next instant, she was reading what was written there.

'Oh no.'

She had spoken aloud and the sound of her own voice brought her to the full realization of what she was reading.

So Kate had known.

It was the one thing which stood out clearly in Lise's mind. Then why had she asked Laura to-night? Lise read the letter again. No name was mentioned. So Kate had merely known that there was *someone*. And, she had to find out who it was. Suddenly Lise understood just how her mother's mind had worked. By including all the attractive women they knew in the party, she would be able to pick the right one as soon as Dell was confronted with her. And, she had done so unerringly. Lise was quite sure of that.

What would Kate do now? Lise

hoped that she would tell Dell, but she rather doubted if Kate's pride would allow her to do that. And, if not? Kate would continue to worry about something which was now nonexistent and the situation would not improve.

Lise longed to be able to tell her mother what she knew, but one thing at least, she understood. More than anything else, Kate would hate her children to know what was happening. Lise stood staring down at the hateful letter on the table feeling entirely helpless. She moved sharply as steps sounded in the hall. Swiftly she folded the letter and thrust it back into the overall pocket, placing it back on the chair. When Kate came through the door, Lise was picking up the plate she had refilled.

'They seem to be enjoying the food. It all seems to be disappearing pretty quickly.'

Kate's voice was bright and Lise had never admired her more. There was no trace in her manner of what she must be feeling. For one mad moment, Lise was tempted to tell her what she knew but caught herself in time. This was something which must remain between her parents.

Busily they stood replenishing further dishes. Both women stood for a moment as they returned to the party, searching for Dell and Lise heard her mother's breath go on a long sigh as she saw him talking to some old friends. Lise noticed that Paul stood unobtrusively behind her father on the edge of the group. He caught her glance and smiled. He was certainly a splendid watch dog and she was grateful. For the first time too, she noticed that he had a nice smile.

Laura left early, obviously disgruntled at the way things had turned out. Possibly she had arrived with the hope that Dell had had second thoughts and had asked Kate to invite her. If so, thought Lise with glee, she must have been singularly disappointed because Dell had made his attitude abundantly clear.

Kate was standing by herself and in a fleeting unguarded moment, Lise saw her defeated expression and it made her heart ache. With newly acquired wisdom, she was convinced that this was something which only concerned her parents and only they themselves could resolve it. The final outcome hinged on whether their love for each other was strong enough to overcome this barrier of misunderstanding.

To Kate, that night seemed endless. Dell touched her as she lay beside him and she cringed away, unable to understand how he could want her when he had been making love to Laura. She heard him sigh as he turned away. Laura — yes — she might have guessed. Laura who was always so gay, so beautiful and so superbly dressed. What chance had she against such strong competition? But this was *Dell*. How could he?

She answered that swiftly. Dell was human, the same as any other man. He was no different. It was only she who had thought he was. It was her mistake for putting him above other men. Her mistake for not being more careful of her own appearance. It had been stupid to think that he was beyond temptation and now she was paying the price for her mistakes. Other women, she knew, turned a blind eye to this kind of thing and continued their marriages on that footing.

Kate lay on her back, trying to imagine her own marriage on that level. Other people accepted second best, why couldn't she? She moved restlessly. Because she still loved Dell. She knew in this moment that curiously, she loved him more than ever before. Which was odd, because when she thought of Laura, she couldn't bear him to touch her.

She thought of that foul letter and how all this could affect his practice. Didn't he care about that either? Everything about this was so unlike the Dell she knew that she felt completely out of her depth. All she could do was relate it to the coming of Paul Quest and what she still thought of as his interference with Johnnie. Johnnie was better; much better. But he didn't need *her* any more. Was that what she resented? For the first time she asked herself the question and was not sure of the answer. But she couldn't blame Paul for this latest development.

Suddenly she wondered how far back the change in Dell had started. Perhaps she had only become aware of change since she had not been so preoccupied with Johnnie. She reminded herself grimly that even now, she only knew about Laura because of the anonymous letter.

Kate turned restlessly in the bed. And now? Her weary mind went round and round the problem. One moment almost deciding to tell Dell that she knew about Laura, the next knowing that her pride would never let her. She couldn't do it because whatever happened, she would never plead for Dell's love. She didn't want him on those terms. It had to be his own free decision.

So, if she didn't intend to sit still and watch her marriage disintegrate, was there any other alternative? Laura was the only one she could think of and the very thought of going to see her turned her cold. She told herself that any such visit would be hopeless. Laura wasn't the sort of woman whose better feelings could be appealed to. Then what? There was nothing else. So, it was just a matter of gathering the necessary courage and Kate wasn't sure if she had enough.

Finally, with nothing settled, she drifted into a troubled uneasy sleep. It was late when she woke and Dell had already gone.

18

That morning, Lise opened her own letters in her little office next to the surgery. One was addressed in odd printed capitals cut from a magazine. She picked it up reluctantly. Another abomination like she had read last night? But it wasn't.

'Darling,'

Philip's clear writing filled the page.

'I am truly sorry. I never meant it to happen like this. I can't go without telling you that in spite of everything at least my love for you was real. It has always been the excitement of this which has got me — the mental exercise of the exact planning, the careful organisation. And the money.

Money means a lot to me. I think you know that.

'You will realise if you have read as far as this that I am putting my safety entirely in your hands. I've no doubt, although I shall be far away by the time you receive this, that the police could trace me if you showed it to them. My future, therefore, is in your hands. Philip.'

Lise was reading it through a second time as Paul came into the office. She remained unaware of him until he moved towards the desk and spoke, then she looked up at him blankly.

'Lise — what is it?'

His eyes went to the letter in her hand, then to the envelope on the desk.

'Philip.' Her voice sounded quite dead. Paul stood without moving. At last, he asked quietly, 'He's coming back?'

She shook her head.

'Not unless — ' She found she couldn't finish the sentence. If she did, she would be committing herself. They stared silently at each other. Finally, as if she had come to a sudden decision, she thrust the letter towards him.

'Please read it. What shall I do?'

Reluctantly taking it from her, Paul read it, put it down on the desk and moved over to the window with his back to her. She watched him, puzzled.

'Paul?'

He turned angrily.

'Why did you show me? Why are you asking *me* what to do? This is for you to decide. *Only* you. Don't you understand?' He raised his hands in a sort of blind protest. 'No one — nobody at all can help you. This is for you.'

She stared at him in the horrified realisation that he spoke the truth. That truth which Philip had stated in his letter, 'I am putting my safety entirely in your hands.'

Her eyes searched Paul's furious face.

'Why are you so angry?'

She didn't know why she asked him this now, when the other thing was so much more important, but oddly, she felt she had to know. He moved impatiently.

'Because he should never have written it. He should never have placed you in such a position.'

Lise said meekly, 'But he need not have written at all. I mean, to tell me he — ' the sentence fell away before Paul's scorn.

'And what was it worth — this so-called love of his? It would have been kinder to leave you with nothing rather than send you this.' He flicked the paper with a scornful finger.

'But he must have loved me to risk writing.'

Paul turned and looked at her.

'*Did* he take any risk?'

Lise stared down at the desk. Had Philip taken any risk? Or was he so sure what she would do?

'Haven't you already made up your mind?'

She put out both hands in a hopeless gesture.

'I don't know. I don't think I have.' And her answer surprised herself. Her feelings for Philip were desperately mixed. Anger, disappointment, disgust and finally, pity were all there. Even the shreds of her own love remained to complicate everything. She saw suddenly that by showing the letter to Paul, she had involved him in this decision between right and wrong. It was easy for him to say that the decision must be hers and hers alone but now, she had entrusted him too with Philip's future. What a fool she had been.

'What are *you* going to do?'

'I told you — the decision is yours.'

'But, *you* know now.'

'What difference does that make?

She said in genuine surprise, 'A big difference. Now that you know, *you* can go to the police.'

'You think I would do that?'

'Why not?'

'Oh, Lise — you don't understand.' He moved impatiently. 'If you decide not to do anything, then — right or wrong — that's the finish.'

'But there's nothing to stop you — '

'Oh yes there is. There's you. Don't you see that you've placed me in exactly the same position in which Philip placed you?'

'You mean, Philip trusted *me* with his future, and now *I*'ve trusted you.'

'Exactly.'

Outside the door, patients were beginning to shuffle into the waiting-room. Paul looked at his watch and walked towards the door.

'Let me know what you decide.'

For one moment, she hesitated, then thrust out her hands in a gesture of defeat.

'I don't think I could live with it if I took this to the police.' Slowly, she picked up the letter, her eyes on Paul's face and, tearing it into several pieces, dropped them into the wastepaper basket.

Paul said sharply, 'No — burn it, and the envelope.'

She looked surprised and he continued quietly, 'Right or wrong, I agree that you couldn't live with it and as far as I am concerned, that is the finish.'

She looked at him gratefully.

'Thank you Paul. You've helped me a lot. Even if you didn't want to,' she added with the trace of a smile.

He held the door open for her and they both went through into the surgery.

Dell had already left by the time Kate came down that morning and, because she was late, she had little time to think of her own troubles. They remained, a hateful nagging grind at the back of her mind, almost deliberately thrust away because she could come to no decision as to what she was going to do.

Putting clean shirts away in Dell's wardrobe, Kate was suddenly aware of Laura's scent on the sleeve of a jacket hanging there. It was curious that such a small thing should give her the necessary courage to call on Laura. Before she could change her mind, she went to put on a coat, discarding her first choice and choosing the new fur one which Dell had given her for her birthday. She made up her face with great care and touched her hair into place. She had to look her best for the ordeal ahead. She couldn't afford to give any points away.

She drove fast, stopping the car by Laura's front door. She rang the bell, waiting with a fast beating heart and trembling hands. The woman from the lodge opened the door and Kate was suddenly aware of the colour draining from the woman's face, and the scared expression in her eyes. With utter certainty, Kate said coldly, 'you wrote that foul letter, didn't you?'

The woman's expression changed, her whole manner becoming belligerent.

'I don't know what you're talking about. You'd better take care what you're saying, the law — '

'I wouldn't mention the law if I were you.'

Kate's voice was filled with angry scorn. 'I'll deal with you later. At the moment, I want to see Mrs. Denham. Please tell her I am here.'

'Well, you can't see 'er. She's in London.' And before Kate could move, the door was slammed in her face. For a moment, she leaned weakly against the pillar beside the door, then went slowly down the steps back to her car.

Driving home, she wondered if she would ever be able to bring her courage to the point of visiting Laura a second time.

At least she had had the satisfaction of tracing the origin of the letter. Although she had no proof, her own conviction was as strong as if she had seen the woman write it. What was she going to do about that? It could wait. There were more important matters to be dealt with in the meantime and she knew that she had frightened the woman badly.

The next time Kate visited Laura, she went in the afternoon and a surprised Laura opened the door. She pulled herself together almost without pause.

'Kate — how nice — come in.'

Kate followed her in, taking a chair which Laura indicated. She began without preface.

'Laura — how *could* you?'

It wasn't what she had meant to say, yet she saw that it had shaken Laura out of her complacency.

'How could I what Kate dear?'

Her voice was artificial but she contrived to look puzzled.

'Surely you don't need to ask that?'

Laura's eyebrows rose in unreal surprise.

'I simply can't imagine what you mean.'

'If that were true, you would be an extremely stupid woman, and you certainly aren't that.'

'How kind Kate.'

The cool, insolent voice gave Kate the necessary impetus to continue. Aware that she was shaking, Kate sat forward, determined to say what she had come to say. She stared at Laura coldly.

'Dell and I have been married a long time. Happily married, which is something I imagine you wouldn't know about, because I understand that your own marriage was not. I believe your husband left you after only two years.'

Laura said angrily, 'I don't know why you have come, but you are being very offensive.'

'But not,' Kate answered quickly, 'as offensive as you who are trying to take my husband away.'

The room was very quiet while she waited for Laura to speak, and she watched her closely, seeing the expressions which flitted across the lovely face. Surprise and dismay that Kate knew; indecision as to how to deal with this unforeseen situation and, finally, open hatred.

'Kate, *dear* — what an imagination! You poor thing. Whatever gave you this absurd idea? Perhaps you aren't well?'

Kate, giving her a withering glance, rose from her chair, taking the anonymous letter from her pocket and holding it out to Laura.

'Read that.'

Laura's surprise was genuine, as was her anger which followed it.

'Where did you get this filth?'

Kate said calmly, 'Your daily woman wrote it.'

'What utter nonsense.'

'Who else would be in a position to know what happened?'

'Nothing happened.'

Laura saw too late what she had admitted.

'Then you don't deny the contents of the letter are true?'

'It didn't happen like that.'

'Then — how did it happen?'

'Dell was attending me professionally.'

Kate remained silent and Laura looked at her contemptuously.

'You don't believe that, do you? But it's true.'

'Oh, I believe it but — ' Kate indicated the letter with a wave of her hand, 'but — champagne and kisses in the bedroom?'

For the first time, Laura had the grace to look uncomfortable.

'I'd been ill. I was better. It was in the nature of a little celebration, that's all.'

'Dell cures a lot of his patients but I doubt if any of them offer him champagne and kisses as a reward.' Kate's voice was icy and Laura turned on her in sudden rage.

'Oh Kate, you fool. Can't you see *why* you've lost him? All that time spent with that stupid boy; never taking any notice of Dell, never taking any trouble with your own looks. Is it any wonder that he's looked elsewhere for his pleasure? No man likes to be ignored, to see a cripple always considered before *him*. Can't you *see* what a fool you've been? You deserve to lose him, you really do.'

This was defeat, and Kate knew it.

She stood up and without looking at Laura, walked out of the house and drove home.

Laura was right and she was wrong. Dell had never agreed with her about Johnnie and he was being proved right. She no longer resented the treatment which was so obviously doing good.

And Dell? If she told him she knew, he would stay with her and on the surface everything would be the same. It wouldn't be enough. Dell must be free to choose, and with a sense of defeat, she wondered how long she could stand this intolerable strain.

19

Paul watched Lise as she cleared up the surgery. She worked automatically, her mind obviously elsewhere, her face pale and drawn.

He said, 'Have you heard any more?'

She shook her head.

'I shan't hear again.' She seemed quite definite and he was inclined to agree with her, saying tentatively, 'He wasn't worth much.'

'No.'

'But you were in love with him, so I suppose that doesn't make much difference.'

Lise placed a pen neatly on the desk.

'I don't think I was in love with him. I couldn't have been to feel as I do now.'

Her head was bent, one finger touching the pen.

'You mean,' Paul asked carefully, 'that

you don't feel as upset as you expected?'

'I mean — I feel free,' she answered quietly. Paul examined the taut, white face.

'Then what *is* worrying you?'

She turned to face him.

'Mother knows. About Dad, I mean.'

'Are you sure?'

She told him about finding the letter and saw him frown.

'Damn. I thought it had all been tied up neatly.'

'You don't think he's still seeing her?'

'I'm certain he isn't. Nor wants to.'

'Oh, Paul, what can I do?'

'You could tell Kate that you saw the letter and that you know there's nothing between Dell and Laura Denham.'

Paul didn't really believe in what he was saying. He knew that Lise would refuse to do anything of the kind.

She shook her head.

'She would hate me to know. I couldn't do that.'

'Then, I think we must wait. I expect Dell will find a way to deal with it.'

'She won't tell him about the letter. I'm quite certain of that,' Lise said with conviction, adding viciously, 'I could kill that woman. I wish she'd go away and leave us alone. The trouble is, she's so damned attractive. I suppose most men would be bowled over.'

Paul smiled.

'Not this one. She's not my type and I don't like the scent she wears.'

'Scent? What's that got to do with it?'

'Oh, a lot. Cloying, like herself you see. You can tell a lot about a woman by the scent she wears.'

He was quite serious and for the first time, Lise smiled.

'And mine?' she couldn't resist asking.

'Clean — peppery — sharp — yes, I like it.'

'I'm honoured.'

He gave her a swift smile before picking up his bag from the desk.

'You should be.' At the door he turned, 'Don't worry too much. We'll work something out.'

Lise called after him, 'Have you got

your boots in the car — the snow's quite deep.'

'No. Thanks for reminding me.'

He went off, whistling, almost child-ishly pleased that she had thought about his needing boots to go out in the snow.

At breakfast next morning, two important letters arrived. The one for Johnnie was from the B.B.C. He held it in his hand for a moment, not daring to open it; thinking he knew only too well what it contained. Finally, he plucked up courage.

'Dear Mr. Manley,

'I have now read the First Act and synopsis of your Play, 'The Narrow Passage'. I think it certainly has possibilities and I would like the opportunity of discussing it with you. Perhaps you could make an appoint-ment to meet me here at your convenience.

Yours sincerely,
M. Clarence.'

Johnnie couldn't believe it. It had been Paul who had suggested he send the First Act and a synopsis before completing the Play. Everything whirled in his excited brain. It was like a sort of magic. The kind of thing which might happen to other people, but never to him. He struggled for calmness.

'Dad, look at this.'

Dell glanced up from his newspaper and was instantly struck by his son's expression. He took the letter from him, reading it carefully, aware that Johnnie was watching him closely. He was also aware that his own emotions were not entirely under control as he handed it back.

'That's terrific, Johnnie. When will you go?'

'I'll have to ring up and find out when he can see me.' Johnnie paused. 'Do you think it really means any-thing?'

Dell looked at the thin, eager face, at that moment understanding something of what this must mean to Johnnie. But what if it didn't mean as much as the boy was hoping? There was nothing definite. But, at this stage, there couldn't be.

He said cautiously, 'He wouldn't suggest seeing you unless he thought something of it.'

'No, that's what I thought.'

'At the same time,' Dell warned, 'we've no experience of how they deal with these things so I suppose it would be wise not to set too much store by this letter. All the same, it's pretty exciting. Congratulations.'

He turned to where Kate had been sitting, surprised that she had not said anything. Surely she wasn't going to disapprove of this. Surely she would be pleased for him. But Kate was disappearing out of the room, almost slamming the door behind her and he looked at it in astonishment.

On the other side of the door Kate stood leaning against it, the letter still in her hand, her heart thudding. Slowly she pushed herself away from the door and went upstairs to the bedroom. This time, the printing had been cut from a magazine.

'You may as well admit that you have lost him and let him have some happiness before it is too late. He doesn't want you. Let him go.'

Nothing more. Kate found that she was shaking. She put the letter down on the dressing-table and started making the bed, wholly unaware of what she was doing, all her mind directed towards the contents of the letter. Yet, other than its beastliness, what difference did it make? Only, she supposed, because it was proof that it was still going on. She was surprised too, that the woman had risked a second letter when she had been accused so directly of having written the first one.

Kate stood frowning down at the blanket she held in her hand, then she went over to the dressing-table, staring at the piece of paper. There was something different here and after a minute, she picked it up, running down the stairs to her desk in the drawing-room. She wasn't even certain that she had kept it and searched frantically through the desk until finally, there it was, Laura's invitation to dinner.

Kate set it beside today's letter. The paper was the same. She picked up first one, then the other. They both smelled of scent. The scent Laura always used. So, it was Laura who had sent this. Laura making a final effort to profit by her daily woman's indiscretion.

Kate sat down suddenly, aware that her legs felt like jelly, her mind whirling. She pressed her fingers over her eyes as if that would enable her to think more clearly.

'Oh — I'm sorry if I'm disturbing you. I just came to tell you how delighted I am with Johnnie's news.'

Paul stood just inside the door. Kate hadn't heard him come and she raised her head to look at him almost without recognition.

'Johnnie's news?'

Paul looked at her quickly.

'What's the matter?'

He came swiftly into the room to stand beside her and she made no attempt to hide the letters.

'I've had a shock,' she said, gesturing towards them.

Quickly Paul glanced at them, then back at Kate.

'An anonymous letter?'

'Yes. The second I've had.'

'You received this one today?'

'Yes. Oh, Paul — what am I going to do?'

Suddenly, she was sobbing, her hands over her face, all her defences down. Paul stood quietly until finally, she took away her hands and looked up at him with her disfigured face.

'What can I do?' she asked again, entirely unconscious of the irony that it was Paul of all men from whom she was seeking help.

'May I read it?'

'Yes. I'll show you the first one.'

She unlocked a drawer in the desk, took out the first letter and placed it beside the other. She watched while Paul read. He studied both letters carefully.

'These are not written by the same person,' he said finally.

'No.'

'You realised that?' He sounded surprised.

Kate indicated Laura's invitation.

'Smell that — and that,' she ordered.

'The same scent,' Paul said. He was treading warily, very conscious that Kate was asking his help merely because he had caught her on the rebound of shock. He was anxious not to frighten her off by letting her think that he had any previous knowledge.

Kate said, 'Laura's scent,' and Paul waited.

'She's trying to take Dell away from me.'

It was almost the cry of a child.

'And you think she could do that?'

Paul's voice was very quiet and it

didn't seem odd to Kate that he had asked the question. 'I think she's already done it,' she said, and the words held tragedy.

'No.'

Kate shook her head.

'Yes — I'm sure. I went to see her and she said I'd lost him, that I deserved to lose him because I put Johnnie first. I — '

'And you believed her — You *believed* that she could do that?'

Kate's surprise was genuine.

'Of course. You see, it was true. I did put Johnnie first. All those years. Johnnie needed me so much.' She paused, making a helpless gesture with both hands. 'I thought so, but he didn't, did he? He really didn't need me at all.'

'Oh yes, he did. He still needs you. It was just that his needs were different from what you thought, but Kate, listen to me. I've something to tell you.'

He took her hands and led her to a more comfortable chair, went over and closed the door, then came and sat down near her. He was finding it difficult to know where to begin. Each person concerned had concealed knowledge from the other. Each had done it for a good purpose, yet nothing had been achieved except further complications. His job was to decide how much he must tell. That this was the moment for truth was apparent but as far as he could see, his own and Lise's knowledge need not be mentioned. It could make no difference and would only distress Kate further. It was only Dell's part which he had to make clear and he was not going to pull any punches over that. If these two were ever going to have any real happiness, everything had to be dealt with now. It was fortunate, he reflected wryly, that it was his day off because this was going to take some time.

'I'd like to start with me,' he said quietly, 'because I know that I was the cause of some of this and I take full responsibility for this.'

He paused, giving her a chance to say

something, but she sat silently, waiting.

'I think Dell's love for you is deeper now than it has ever been.'

Kate made an impatient gesture and he put up a hand.

'You must believe that because it is true. It is also true that he doesn't care a damn about Laura and never has done. You must believe that as well.'

Her eyes were scornful as she watched him, afraid to believe and thinking that he was only trying to comfort her. He went on to describe that first visit of Dell's to Laura as Dell himself had described it to him, he tried to make her feel and understand Dell's desperate unhappiness and what had been done to him, and the silent woman opposite him began to relax and listen more attentively and when finally, he looked at her, he saw the tears that ran slowly down her face. Paul let out a long sigh. He had won.

Sitting quietly, he gave her time to recover; time to understand that she and Dell could have a life again, perhaps a better one than ever before. Because she had grieved so bitterly, the knowledge was slow to sink in and he allowed her plenty of time during which he gave a lot of thought to the problem of Laura. He recollected Lise saying, 'I wish she'd go away.' That, of course, would be the ideal answer. But how to achieve it? Gradually a scheme presented itself to him, but it would have to depend entirely on Kate. She must have the final say.

Kate said, 'I hate to think of that woman getting off scot free.'

'It's up to you whether she does or not.'

'How?' Kate watched him closely.

'I can tell you how I think it can be done. It is only a question of what you want.'

For the first time, Kate smiled.

'I'm only human,' she said mildly. 'I don't pretend to be a saint. I'm afraid I'd like to see her suffer a bit.'

'Laura has to be thoroughly frightened,' Paul began with relish. Kate sat forward in her chair, eager to hear what he had to propose. When he had finished, he said, 'and so, if you will let me have the letters, I will do the rest.'

Smiling at him, Kate shook her head.

'Oh no, you're not going to do that.'

Paul shrugged.

'If you want to try and get her out of your hair, it's the only way.'

'Oh, I agree, only *I'm* the one who is going to see her — not you.'

Paul was taken by surprise. This was something he hadn't expected.

'*You* can't do it Kate.'

'Oh yes, I can. It will be some recompense for the misery she has put me through. But Dell musn't know until afterwards.'

'Kate — I wish you wouldn't. I don't like this.'

She stood up.

'It may take all the courage I have,' she said with a smile, 'but it will be worth it and it is something I must do — something I *want* to do.' She put a hand lightly on his shoulder. 'I don't think you can know how much you have done for me today, but thank you and — ' she hesitated, even now finding it difficult to say. 'And thank you too, for what you have done for Johnnie. It's rather odd, isn't it, that you and I should end up as allies.'

Paul burst out laughing. 'Well, I must admit that I never visualised anything like that happening, but may I say I'm very glad that it has?'

'You may, and I'm delighted.'

They stood facing each other for a moment before he left her and already he could see the change in her. It was almost as if she were coming to life again. She put up a hand to her face, thinking his gaze was a criticism.

'I know I must look terrible.'

He shook his head.

'As a matter of fact, you look better than you have for a long time. You look alive again.'

Realising what he meant, she gave

him an appreciative smile.

'I am, but all the same, I'm not going to Laura's looking like this.'

'That's the spirit — bib and tucker and sally forth bravely.'

20

After a careful make-up routine, Kate slipped into her fur coat and, downstairs, picking up the two letters, put them in her pocket.

It was snowing hard and Kate drove carefully, skidding down the unsanded lane to the main road. Seeing that Laura's drive was deep in snow, she left the car outside. Curiously, she felt perfectly calm and capable of dealing with this situation. She rang the bell, stepping inside as soon as Laura opened the door.

'Kate — what a surprise — well — come in, of course.'

Kate followed her into the drawing-room and stood facing her. 'This is not a social visit, as you must realise. I came to offer you the choice of what to do.'

Laura's usual poise was missing. This

visit was quite unexpected, Kate's manner so assured that she could make no assessment. She said tentatively, 'What I will do? I don't understand.'

'I'm sure you don't,' Kate said blandly, 'I'll explain. There are two alternatives. You can either go away at once, or stay and face the police.'

Kate watched Laura's colour recede, saw her struggle for recovery.

'I can't imagine what you are talking about.' Laura managed to make her voice cool and sharp but Kate detected the beginning of fear in her eyes and felt a quick stab of pleasure.

'I can't,' she said pleasantly, 'believe your imagination is so faulty, however, it is easy to explain. I received — as you are aware — a second anonymous letter today and — '

'You think it's that wretched woman again?' Laura looked momentarily relieved.

'No. I know it isn't.'

Laura looked at Kate who outstared her and Laura's eyes flickered away.

'Then — who do you think wrote it?'

She turned to a chair. 'We may as well sit down.'

'*You* wrote it.'

There was an appreciable silence before Laura said too loudly, 'How absurd. Why would I do that?'

Standing looking down at her, Kate saw her hands were shaking. The sight pleased her but she remembered Paul's warning. 'Go carefully, you're not in a strong position. It just depends on how much you can frighten her.'

'It was a last desperate try to make me think that Dell was unfaithful to me. You thought that if I believed that, I wouldn't want him any more, and that would be your chance.' Kate drew a deep breath. 'There is only one thing you didn't allow for. Dell doesn't want you.'

She hoped that was true as she watched the anger in Laura's eyes.

'You're a fool if you think that,' she said viciously. 'He wanted me all right,' she looked at Kate contemptuously. 'He hadn't the guts to break clear; that's all.'

Kate tried to hold on to her temper as she took out the letters.

'I have plenty of proof who wrote that letter. I imagine you aren't very practised in writing anonymous letters. You made the mistake of using your own notepaper.'

There was a long silence.

'What rubbish. My notepaper comes from a general supplier, and anyone can buy it.'

Kate's voice was calm and sure as she said, 'You've always told me your notepaper comes from London. Always the same — a very pale blue.' She shrugged. 'But what finally clinches it is that you always wear a distinctive scent.' She named it and Laura frowned.

'What can scent have to do with an anonymous letter?' she asked contemptuously, but Kate heard the note of doubt. She unfolded the two letters, holding them for Laura to see.

'Both these reek of the scent you use. Those two things taken together are rather too much of a coincidence, don't you think?'

Laura glared silently at the letters.

'Let me look at them,' she held out her hand but Kate shook her head. 'You can see them quite clearly from here. One, as you see, is your invitation to dinner, the other, the one I received this morning.'

'You think the police would be interested in those?'

In spite of the scathing tones, Kate knew she had won. Laura, who doubtless knew as little about law as Kate, was frightened. Kate followed up her advantage.

'I'm sure they would. Particularly as it concerns a doctor. As you know, I am in the strong position of being able to tell them who wrote the letters. Which is what matters.'

Laura said blusteringly, 'You wouldn't dare take this rubbish to the police. They'd laugh at you.'

Kate folded the letters and returned them to her pocket.

'It's quite easy to find out, isn't it? It's a risk I'm quite willing to take.'

She started walking to the door, turning as she reached it.

'I will give you plenty of time to make your decision,' she said kindly. 'But if at the end of three days you haven't left here, I shall take the letters to the police and from then on, they will be dealing with it.'

She turned as she reached the door.

'Don't bother to get up, I'll let myself out.' She closed the door softly behind her.

Outside, the sudden freezing cold and blinding snow made her feel lightheaded and as she floundered down the drive, she felt as if she were walking above the ground; it gave her a queer sensation of triumph.

Her windscreen was blocked with snow which had to be cleared before she could start and she had difficulty in controlling the car as it skidded on the freezing road. In spite of these difficulties, she felt a lot happier. Whatever Laura's final decision, Kate knew she had nothing to fear from her.

The whirling snow obliterated the turning into the lane until she had almost passed it. Instinctively, she applied the brakes and turned the wheel. The car skidded across the lane, ploughed through the hedge and tilted wildly into the ditch.

Kate, aware of sharp pain in her wrist and the fact that she had banged her head, switched off the engine and sat staring at the field beyond. The car gave a lurch and one wheel sank firmly to the bottom of the ditch, sliding Kate across the seat. Cautiously she pulled herself back, wondering how she was going to get out of this crazy car. Finally, she managed to get the door open and drop into deep snow and, soaked, she trudged back to the house which she knew would be empty at this time.

Her head throbbing and her wrist

already swelling and painful, she somehow managed to change her wet clothes
and, shivering with cold, huddled in
front of the study fire. Her wrist, she
thought, was broken but there was
nothing she could do about it until
somebody came, so she sat back trying
to ignore the pain and to concentrate
on her confrontation with Laura. She
thought ruefully that she had committed herself. If Laura hadn't gone in
three days, she would have to contact
the police, something she was reluctant
to do.

21

'Kate — Kate? Where are you?'

In spite of the pain, she must have dozed and the urgent sound of Dell's voice roused her. For a moment, she couldn't think what had happened or why Dell should be shouting for her with that note of fear in his voice. She sat up stiffly.

'I'm here Dell. In the study.'

He came blundering in as if he had all hell after him, stopping abruptly as he saw her.

'Kate — Kate darling, what happened? I saw the car and you weren't there and I thought — ' he broke off with an expressive gesture. 'I don't know what I thought. Thank God you're here.'

He came to kneel beside her and she held out her wrist.

'I took a bang on my head and I

think this is broken, but otherwise, I'm all right.'

She watched his shaking fingers as gently he examined her wrist. She let her eyes rest on his anxious face, exulting in this feeling of closeness.

He said crossly, 'Did you *have* to go out on a day like this? You might have been killed.'

'Yes, I had to go out,' she answered and met his worried eyes.

'Oh, Kate.'

She leaned forward to kiss him.

'I'm here,' she said gently, 'don't worry; I'm all right.'

Suddenly he smiled and stood up.

'I'll fetch your coat, I must get you to hospital, that wrist's broken.'

He brought her back from the hospital some hours later, the pain reasonable now that the wrist was in plaster. She watched him move round the room, pulling curtains, making up the fire. She was aware that his manner had changed. There had been that moment of closeness borne of his fear for her safety; a moment in which he had shown her his love, but now that moment had gone as if it had never been and she was conscious of a feeling of renewed strain between them.

He said as he threw on a log, 'Paul wanted me to tell you that he was sorry about your accident but that he hopes you had had a successful day. I don't know what he meant. Perhaps you do.'

He sounded disgruntled but Kate couldn't help smiling.

'Yes, I know what he means,' she said. 'Is he coming in tonight?'

'No.' His tone was terse and again she wondered what had happened. He turned at the door.

'You'll be all right until I'm through surgery?'

Kate smiled at him.

'Quite all right.'

He went out without returning her smile, closing the door behind him. Although Kate could not account for his change of manner, she was not greatly worried by it. Quiet in her mind with the certainty of his love, there were now no barriers which could not be broken down between them. There was nothing which could not finally be resolved. She waited peacefully by the fire for his return.

After a cold supper which he insisted on preparing, they sat in the comfortably warm room and Kate asked him about the car which had been towed to a garage.

'The chap said it would be about a week. In any case, you won't be able to drive. You'll have to get Johnnie to drive you.'

'Where did you say Johnnie was?'

'He's having dinner with Paul to celebrate.'

Suddenly, Kate remembered.

'His news? What was it? Celebrating what?'

'Of course — you never heard. He had a letter from the B.B.C. about his Play. They want to see him. They think it has possibilities.'

'Why, Dell, that's wonderful. Do you

think they're going to take it? You know, I never thought he would be able to — '

Kate stopped in mid-sentence, then, looking at Dell, accepted complete defeat.

'I was wrong, wasn't I? Wrong about everything.'

For answer, he said, 'It's working out. He's doing splendidly.'

'Yes, I know,' Kate said meekly and there was a long silence, then Dell stood up abruptly, putting his hand in his pocket and bringing out two pieces of paper. He came to stand close to her, holding them out.

'These were found in the car.'

Kate stared unbelievingly.

'They were in my pocket.'

'Then, they must have fallen out.'

Kate put out her hand and he gave them to her.

After a long silence, he said, 'I read them.'

She didn't answer and after a moment, he said, 'I wondered at first what Laura's dinner invitation was doing there. It didn't take me long to work out the inference. She uses a very distinctive scent.'

He watched Kate's bent head.

'Laura sent the other one too, didn't she?'

'Yes.'

He moved sharply away from her.

'Was it the first?'

'The first from Laura.'

He turned quickly.

'You mean, you had another?'

'From that woman at the lodge who works for her.'

Dell had a sudden vivid picture in his mind of that stupid scene in the bedroom and anger flooded through him, in that moment realising what Kate must have been through.

'Kate — did you believe it?'

'At first, I did. And Dell — I deserved it. I've been such a fool all these years. I've been so wrong.' She paused and for the first time, looked up at him. 'But I've always loved you.'

He smiled down at her.

'That makes two of us.'

She nodded.

'Yes. I know that now.'

'How long?'

'How long have I been sure of your love?'

For the first time, she returned his smile.

'Only today.' For a second, she hesitated, then added quietly, 'Paul told me.'

The irony of that didn't escape him, but at this moment nothing mattered but themselves.

'Kate, I've never loved any woman but you, and I never will, so keep that closely in your mind from now on. Now tell me where you went today.'

She answered him meekly.

'I went to Laura's. With the letters.'

He looked at her in amazement as she continued quietly.

'I gave her three days to make up her mind to get out.'

It sounded so unbelievable, so unlike Kate that he almost smiled. He said after a moment, 'Did you give her an alternative?'

'I told her that if she didn't, I would take the letters to the police.'

He searched her face curiously, seeing an expression of grim determination there.

'But darling, you've a pretty thin case.'

Suddenly, she smiled.

'Oh yes, I know. The point is that I was able to frighten her. I don't think she will dare risk it.'

'You sound very complacent.'

Kate frowned.

'Perhaps too complacent. Perhaps, after all, she won't go. Then, I'll have to go to the police.'

'You really would?'

'Yes. I really would.'

After a minute, she said, 'Don't let's think of that tonight. I'm so happy. I don't want to think of anything but us.'

He looked at her white, drawn face.

'You must be in a lot of pain and you've had one hell of a day. You ought to be in bed.'

Suddenly, she laughed.

'I've had the best day for a long time, and I'm not going to bed until the others come in.'

He didn't argue with her, understanding what she meant and they sat quietly talking, relaxed and happy until presently they heard Johnnie and Lise come in.

Lise said as she came through the door, 'I didn't think Johnnie would be able to get to the station, it's still snowing.' She broke off abruptly. 'What have you done to your arm?'

'She took the corner of the lane too fast and ended up in the ditch.'

Her father spoke almost gaily, as if it were something to be proud of and she looked from one to the other in surprise, aware that the atmosphere between her parents was entirely changed and, in spite of Kate's accident, it was impossible not to see that they were happy just to be together. When Johnnie appeared after putting the car away, they heard the details of the accident and both assumed that their mother had been out on a shopping expedition, so no further explanations were necessary.

Kate continued to refuse to go to bed until she had heard about Johnnie's Play.

'I've an appointment next week, so keep your fingers crossed until then.'

The next morning, Lise turned eagerly as Paul entered the surgery.

'Paul — something's happened.'

'Kate's wrist, you mean?'

She shook her head.

'No. Not that. Something's happened between Mother and Dad. They were quite different last night, as if — ' she hesitated, 'as if they suddenly understood each other. I can't explain.'

She looked at him as he stood by his desk, suddenly aware of the smug expression flitting across his face.

'Paul — you know something, don't you?'

He shook his head.

'No. Not that part, but it looks as if — ' he broke off then met her eyes.

'Kate had another letter.'

'Oh, no!'

He looked at his watch.

'Sit down a moment and I'll tell you.'

'And so,' he said as he finished, 'Kate turned sleuth and decided to visit Laura and call her bluff. With what result, I don't know for what with one thing and another, I've not seen her.'

'Was it you who suggested her seeing Laura?'

'Certainly not. I suggested going myself. I didn't want *Kate* to do it.'

Lise wondered as she listened why she had ever thought this man arrogant and she suddenly realised how much he had done for them all as a family. He was saying now with a smile, 'But she insisted on going herself. I really believe she was looking forward to it and I certainly would have liked to be there to hear her.'

He stood up as he heard footsteps in the waiting-room.

'So, I think we've won. At least we're over the worst.'

Lise said impulsively, 'Oh, Paul, you've been so good. Thank you for all you've done.'

It astonished her to see the quick pleasure in his face and surprised herself at the warm feeling that gave her. She hadn't realised how much she herself had come to rely on him, or how much she looked forward each day to working with him.

He turned away quickly, reaching for the white jacket he wore for surgery.

'We're late,' he said tersely, and gestured to the waiting-room door.

★   ★   ★

'Kate? Kate?'

Dell was in the hall and Kate heard the eagerness in his voice as she went out to him.

'Kate — she's gone. You're a clever girl, aren't you?'

He looked at her, savouring this moment which was probably one of the most important in his life. Her face was a little flushed from cooking, her hair a trifle untidy and he thought he had never seen her look so well. He watched her smile spread.

'Oh, Dell. It's over. I can't believe it. That's wonderful.'

He went to take her in his arms, complaining bitterly that he couldn't get near her because of her plastered arm. With one arm round her, he steered her into the study. 'I think we desire a drink,' he said and gave her one.

She smiled up at him as she knelt before the fire.

'Paul was the clever one. He thought of doing it this way.'

'I know, but you had the courage to carry it out.'

'I was playing for big stakes.'

He wondered if she had been as doubtful of the success of her tactics as he had been. He hadn't really believed that Laura would be frightened away by Kate. Perhaps, he thought now, it took women to deal with a situation like this.

Kate had obviously convinced Laura that she would go to the police and rather than face that, she had gone away. For how long, he wondered? But that could wait. At the moment, he felt intense relief, seeing what lay ahead of them as the chance of a new life with endless possibilities. He held out his hands and helped her up.

'It's all right Kate, isn't it?'

'It's all right, Dell.' She met his eyes seriously but her mouth smiled happily. 'We have so much; we're so lucky.' He held up his glass and they both drank. She said after a moment, 'You know, I think I'm a little tight. I'm not used to drinking at this time of the day. And another thing, I wouldn't be surprised if the lunch is burning,' but she made no attempt to leave him. They were both at peace and it seemed a pity to shorten this moment of quiet happiness between them. Finally, she moved towards the door.

'Dell, you don't think — I mean, you don't suppose Paul — ' She stopped in mid-sentence, finding herself unable to put into words the nebulous thought in her mind.

Dell regarded her gravely.

'Well, I do, actually, though of course, it takes two to make a bargain.'

Kate looked genuinely surprised.

'But I didn't finish what I was going to say.'

'You didn't need to. You're fairly transparent as far as I'm concerned.'

'Then, what *did* you mean?'

'Only that I know that Paul is in love with Lise, but as I said, it takes two to make a bargain.'

THE END